"You Never Really Knew Anything About Me, Except That You Liked To Kiss Me," She Told Him.

"The first time I kissed you, you gasped under my mouth," he recalled quietly. "It surprised me that you didn't know what a deep kiss felt like."

Her green eyes glittered at him angrily. "There's no need to rub it in."

"If you hadn't been a virgin, our lives would have been a lot different," he continued. "I wanted you so badly that I couldn't think straight, but you were the original old-fashioned girl. No sex before marriage."

"I'm still the original old-fashioned woman," she told him proudly. "My body is my business. I can do whatever I want to with it, and that includes being celibate if I feel like it."

"Nights must get real cold in the winter," he chided.

Her eyebrows lifted. "I have an electric blanket. How about you?"

Dear Reader,

Happy New Year! The New Year means new beginnings, a renewed sense of purpose. It also means New Year resolutions, and I have one I want to share with all of you.

I resolve to continue to bring you the sexiest, sassiest, most sparkling love stories around. In the upcoming year, you'll see books both from new authors and your special favorites. These writers are committed to creating wonderful romances filled with love and laughter, tears and joys, and to inventing heroes who will fulfill your every fantasy.

I also resolve to continue to publish books filled with variety. Six Desire books are available for you each and every month, and you, as readers, should expect that the stories have difference and diversity. So expect a fabulous mix of traditional stories and bold, innovative plot lines.

Silhouette Desire is ever-changing and ever-challenging. But the one thing that will never change is its quality. I thank you all for your continued support throughout the years, because without the readers there wouldn't be Silhouette Desire!

Sincerely,

Lucia Macro
Silhouette Desire

Please address questions and book requests to:
Reader Service
U.S.: P.O. Box 1325, Buffalo, NY 14269
Canadian: P.O. Box 1050, Niagara Falls, Ont. L2E 7G7

DIANA PALMER
SECRET AGENT MAN

SILHOUETTE *Desire*®

Published by Silhouette Books

America's Publisher of Contemporary Romance

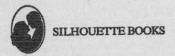 **SILHOUETTE BOOKS**

ISBN 0-373-05829-2

SECRET AGENT MAN

Copyright © 1994 by Diana Palmer

Printed in U.S.A.

Books by Diana Palmer

Silhouette Desire

The Cowboy and the Lady #12
September Morning #26
Friends and Lovers #50
Fire and Ice #80
Snow Kisses #102
Diamond Girl #110
The Rawhide Man #157
Lady Love #175
Cattleman's Choice #193
The Tender Stranger #230
Love by Proxy #252
Eye of the Tiger #271
Loveplay #289
Rawhide and Lace #306
Rage of Passion #325
Fit for a King #349
Betrayed by Love #391
Enamored #420
Reluctant Father #469
Hoodwinked #492
His Girl Friday #528
Hunter #606
Nelson's Brand #618
The Best Is Yet To Come #643
‡*The Case of the Mesmerizing Boss* #702
‡*The Case of the Confirmed Bachelor* #715
‡*The Case of the Missing Secretary* #733
Night of Love #799
Secret Agent Man #829

Silhouette Special Edition

Heather's Song #33
The Australian #239

Silhouette Romance

Darling Enemy #254
Roomful of Roses #301
Heart of Ice #314
Passion Flower #328
Soldier of Fortune #340
After the Music #406
Champagne Girl #436
Unlikely Lover #472
Woman Hater #532
Calhoun #580
Justin #592
Tyler #604
Sutton's Way #670
Ethan #694
Connal #741
Harden #783
Evan #819
Donavan #843
Emmett #910
King's Ransom #971

Silhouette Books

Silhouette Christmas Stories 1987
 "The Humbug Man"
Silhouette Summer Sizzlers 1990
 "Miss Greenhorn"
To Mother with Love 1993
 "Calamity Mom"

Also by Diana Palmer

Diana Palmer Duets Books I-VI
Diana Palmer Collection

‡Most Wanted Series
*Long, Tall Texans

One

Lang Patton felt absolutely undressed without his credentials and the small automatic weapon he'd grown used to carrying on assignment. It had been his own choice to leave the CIA and take a job with a private security company in San Antonio. He was hoping that he wasn't going to regret it.

He walked into the San Antonio airport—weary from the delayed Washington, D.C., flight—with a carryon bag and looked around for his brother Bob.

He was tall and big, dark-eyed and dark-haired, with a broad, sexy face. His brother was an older version of him, but much slighter in build. Bob approached him with a grin, a young boy of six held firmly by the hand.

"Hi," Bob greeted him. "I hope you just got here. I had to bring Mikey with me."

The towheaded boy grinned up at him. He had a front tooth missing. "Hi, Uncle Lang, been shooting any bad guys?" he asked loudly, causing a security man who was talking to a woman at the information counter to turn his head with a suspicious scowl.

"Not lately, Mikey," Lang replied. He shook his brother's hand and bent to lift Mikey up onto his shoulder. "How's it going, pardner?" he asked the boy.

"Just fine! The dentist says I'm going to get a new tooth, but the Tooth Fairy left me a whole dollar for my old one!"

"Just between us, the Tooth Fairy's going bust," Bob said in a lowered voice.

"Can I see your gun, Uncle Lang, huh?" Mikey persisted.

The security guard lifted both eyebrows. Lang could have groaned out loud as the man approached. He'd been through the routine so often that he just put Mikey down and opened his jacket without being asked to.

The security man cocked his head. "Nice shirt, or are you showing off your muscles?"

"I'm showing you that I don't have a gun," Lang muttered.

"Oh, that. No, I wasn't looking for a gun. You're Lang Patton?"

Lang blinked. "Yes."

"Nobody else here fits the description," the man added sheepishly. "Well, there's a Mrs. Patton on the phone who asks that you stop by the auto parts place and pick her up a new carburetor for a '65 Ford Mustang, please."

"No, he will not," Bob muttered. "I told her she can't do that overhaul, but she won't listen. She's going to prove me wrong or...cowardly woman, to sucker *you* into it," he added indignantly to Lang, who was grinning from ear to ear.

"His wife—my sister-in-law—is a whiz with engines," Lang told the security man. "She can fix anything on wheels. But he—" he jerked his thumb at an outraged Bob "—doesn't think it's ladylike."

"What century is he living in?" the security man asked. "Gee, my wife keeps our washing machine fixed. Saves us a fortune in repair bills. Nothing like a wife who's handy with equipment. You should count your blessings," he added to Bob. "Do you know what a mechanic charges?"

"Yes, I know what a mechanic charges, I'm married to one," Bob said darkly. "She owns her own repair shop, and she doesn't care that I don't like her covered in grease and smelling of burned rubber. All I am these days is a glorified baby-sitter."

Lang knew why Bob was upset. He and his brother had spent their childhood playing second fiddle to their mother's job. "You know Connie loves you," he said, trying to pacify Bob. "Besides, you're a career man yourself, and a terrific surveyor," Lang argued when the security man was called away to a passenger in distress. "Mikey will take after you one day. Won't you, Mikey?" he asked the child.

"Not me. I want to be a grease monkey, just like my mommy!"

Bob threw up his hands and walked away, leaving Lang and Mikey to catch up.

The Pattons lived in Floresville, a pleasant little ride down from San Antonio, past rolling land occupied by grazing cattle and oil pumping stations. This part of Texas was still rural, and Lang remembered happy times as a boy when he and Bob visited their uncle's ranch and got to ride horses with the cowboys. Things at home were less pleasant.

"Time passes so quickly," Lang remarked.

"You have no idea," Bob replied. He glanced at Lang. "I saw Kirry downtown the other day."

Lang's heart jumped. He hadn't expected to hear her name mentioned. In five years, he'd done his best to forget her. The memories were sudden and acute, Kirry with her long wavy blond hair blowing in the breeze, her green eyes wide and bright with laughter and love. There were other memories, not so pleasant, of Kirry crying her eyes out and begging a recalcitrant Lang to listen. But he wouldn't. He'd caught her in a state of undress with his best friend and, in a jealous rage, he'd believed the worst. It had taken six months for him to find out that his good friend had set Kirry up because he wanted her for himself.

"I tried to apologize once," Lang said without elaborating, because Bob knew the whole story.

"She won't talk about you to this day," was the quiet reply. Bob turned into the side street that led to the Patton house. "She's very polite when you're mentioned, but she always changes the subject."

"She went away to college before I left," Lang reminded him.

"Yes, and graduated early, with honors. She's vice president of a top public relations firm in San Antonio. She makes very good money, and she travels a lot."

"Does she still come home?" Lang asked.

Bob shook his head. "She avoids Floresville like the plague. She can afford to since her mother sold the old homestead." His eyes shifted to Lang. "You must have hurt her a lot."

Lang smiled with self-contempt. "You have no idea how much."

"It was right after that when you were accepted for the CIA."

"I'd applied six months before," he reminded Bob. "It wasn't a sudden decision."

"It was one you hadn't shared with any of us."

"I knew you wouldn't like it. But here I am, back home and safe, with some pretty exciting memories," Lang reminisced.

"As alone as when you left." Bob indicated Mikey, who was lying down on the back seat of Bob's Thunderbird, reading a Marvel comic book. "If you'd gotten married, you could have had one of those by now."

Lang looked at Mikey and his eyes darkened. "I don't have your courage," he said curtly.

Bob glanced at him. "And you said I shouldn't let the past ruin my life."

Lang shrugged. "It tends to intrude. Less since I've been away."

"But you still haven't coped with it, Lang, you're getting older. You'll want a wife and a family one day."

Lang couldn't argue with wanting a wife. It was the thought of a child that made him hesitate. "My last case reminded me of how short life can be, and how unpredictable," he said absently. "The woman I was helping guard had a kid brother who'd been in a coma for years. He's older than Mikey, but a real nice kid. I got attached to him." He stretched and leaned his head back against the seat. "I did a lot of thinking about where my life was going, and I didn't like what I saw. So when an old friend of mine mentioned this security chief job, I decided to give it a try."

"What old friend?" Bob asked dryly. "Someone female?"

Lang glowered at him. "Yes."

"And still interested in you?"

"Lorna gave me up years ago, before I started going with Kirry. She was only thinking that I might like a change," he said. "It's nothing romantic."

Bob didn't say anything, but his expression did. "Okay, I'll quit prying. Where is it that you're going to work?"

"A corporation called Lancaster, Inc., in San Antonio. It has several holdings, and I'll be responsible for overseeing security in all of them."

Bob made a sound in his throat.

"What was that?" Lang asked curiously.

Bob coughed, choking. "Why, not a thing in this world!" he said. He was grinning. "I hope you like pancakes for dinner, it's all I can cook, and Connie won't be in for hours yet. I usually make her an omelet when she gets here." His hands tightened on the steering wheel. "I hate mechanics!"

"You knew Connie had this talent when you married her ten years ago," Lang reminded him.

"Well, I didn't know she planned to open her own shop, did I? For the past six months, ever since she went into business, I've been living like a single parent! I do everything for Mikey, everything, and she's never home!"

Lang's eyebrows lifted. "Does she have any help?"

"Can't afford any, she says," he muttered darkly, pulling into the driveway of the stately old Victorian house they lived in. Out back was a new metal building, from which loud mechanical noises were emanating.

The elderly lady next door, working in her flowers, gave Bob an overly sweet smile. "How nice to see *you* again, Lang," she said. "I hope you didn't come home for some peace and quiet, because if you did, you'll find more peace and quiet in downtown San Antonio than you'll get here!''

''You're screaming, Martha,'' Bob said calmly.

''I have to scream to be heard with that racket going on night and day!'' the white-haired little lady said. Her face was turning red. ''Can't you make her quit at a respectable hour?''

''Be my guest,'' Bob invited.

''Not me,'' she mumbled, shifting from one foot to the other. ''Tried it once. She flung a wrench at me.'' She made a sniffling noise and went back to work in her flowers.

Lang was trying hard not to laugh. He took his flight bag, and Mikey, out of the back seat.

''Is that all you have?'' Bob asked for the third time since he'd gotten his brother off the plane.

''I don't accumulate things,'' Lang told him. ''It's not sensible when your assignments take you all over the country and around the world.''

''I guess so. You don't accumulate people, either, do you?'' he added sadly.

He clapped a big hand on his brother's shoulder. ''Family's different.''

Bob smiled lopsidedly. ''Yeah.''

''I'll just go out and say hello to Connie.''

''Uh, Lang...''

''It's all right, I'm a trained secret agent,'' Lang reminded him dryly.

"Watch your head. Place is loaded with wrenches...."

Lang banged on the door and waited for the noise to cease and be replaced with loud mutters.

The door was thrown open and a slight woman with brown hair wearing stained blue coveralls and an Atlanta Braves cap peered up at him. "Lang? Lang!"

She hurled herself into his big arms and hugged him warmly. "How are you? When Bob told me you'd given up the Agency to work in San Antonio, I stood up and cheered! Listen, when you get a car, I'll do all your mechnical work free. You can stay with us—"

"No, I can't," he told her. "I have to be in San Antonio, but I can come and visit often, and I will. I'll get a nice big apartment and some toys for Mikey to play with when you bring him up to see me."

She grimaced. "I don't have a lot of time, you know. So many jobs and only me to do them. I can't complain, though, work is booming. We have a new VCR and television set, and Mikey has loads of toys. I even bought Bob a decent four-wheel drive to use in his work." She beamed. "Not bad, huh?"

"Not bad at all," he agreed, wondering if it would be politic to mention that gifts weren't going to replace the time she spent with her family. He and Bob had scars that Connie might not even know about. God knew, Lang had never been able to share his with Kirry, as close as they'd been.

"Well, back to work. Bob's cooking tonight, he'll feed you. I'll see you later, Lang. Did you get me the carburetor?"

He flushed.

She glowered. "Bob, right? He wouldn't let you." She stamped her foot. "I don't know why in heaven's name I had to marry a male chauvinist pig! He looked perfectly sane when I said yes." She turned and went back into the garage, closing the door behind her, still muttering. Lang was certain then that Bob had never shared the past with her.

"Well, did she scream about the carburetor?" Bob asked hopefully as he dished up black-bottomed pancakes in the kitchen.

"Yes."

"Did she tell you how much stuff she's bought us all?" he added. "Nice, isn't it? If we only had her to share it with, it might mean something. Poor old Mikey doesn't even get a bedtime story anymore because she's too tired to read him one. I even do that."

"Have you tried talking to her?" Lang asked.

"Sure. She doesn't listen. She's too busy redesigning engine systems and important stuff like that." He put some pancakes down in front of Mikey, who made a face. "Scrape off the burned part," he instructed his son.

"There's a hamburger from yesterday in the refrigerator. Can't I have that instead?" Mikey asked plaintively.

"Okay. Heat it up in the microwave." Bob grumbled.

"Thanks, Dad! Can I go watch television while I eat?"

"You might as well. Family unity's gone to hell around here."

Mikey whooped and went to retrieve his hamburger from the refrigerator. He heated it up and vanished into his room.

"Poor kid. His cholesterol will be as high as a kite and he'll die of malnutrition."

Lang was staring at the black pancakes. "If he doesn't starve first."

"I can't cook. She didn't marry me for my cooking skills. She should have found somebody who was a gourmet chef in his spare time."

"Why don't you hire a cook?" Lang suggested.

Bob brightened. "Say, that's an idea. We've got plenty of money, so why don't I? I'll start looking tomorrow." He stared at the black pancakes on his own plate and pushed them away. "Tell you what, I'll run down to the corner and get us a couple of Mama Lou's barbecue sandwiches and some fries, how about that?"

Lang grinned. "That's more like it." He paused. "While you're at it, you might tell Connie exactly why you don't like working mothers. If she understood, she might compromise."

"Her? Dream on. And I don't like talking about the past. Go ahead," he suggested when Lang paused. "Tell me you ever said anything to Kirry."

Lang didn't have a comeback. He shrugged and walked away.

He spent a lazy two days with Bob and Connie and Mikey, trying not to notice the disharmony. If the couple hadn't each been so individually stubborn, things might have worked out better. But neither one was going to give an inch or compromise at all.

Before Lang left for San Antonio to see his new boss the following Monday, Bob had interviewed four women to housekeep and cook for the family. The one he favored was a Mexican-American girl who had beautiful black hair down to her waist and soft brown eyes like velvet. Her voice was seductive and she had a figure that made Lang's pulse run wild. This was going to mean trouble, he thought, but he couldn't interfere. His brother had to lead his own life.

Lancaster, Inc., was owned by a middle-aged man and his wife, a fashion-conscious socialite. Although public shares were issued, it was basically a family-held company, and Lang liked the owners at first sight. They were straightforward about his duties and salary, and they made him feel welcome.

He was introduced to his immediate staff, a veteran ex-cop and a woman who was ex-military, two very capable individuals who had been running the operation since the previous security chief left because he couldn't take the pressure.

"Couldn't stand the sight of blood," Edna Riley said with faint contempt. She looked at Lang curiously. "I hear you were CIA."

He nodded. "That's right."

"And before that?"

"I was a street cop on the San Antonio police force."

Edna grinned. "Well, well."

Tory Madison grinned, too. "Sure, I remember you," he said. "I retired about the same time you joined. But I couldn't stay quit. Inactivity was killing me. I can't keep up with the younger ones, but I know a few things that help keep the greenhorns out of trouble. I'm administrative, but that's okay. I like my job."

Lang smiled at him. "When I've had time to look over the operation, I may have some changes in mind. Nothing drastic," he said when they looked worried, "like sweeping the ranks clean and starting over, so don't worry about that, okay?"

They all relaxed. "Okay."

"But we do need to keep up with new methods in the business," he added. "I'm pretty up-to-date on that since I've just come back from the front."

"We'd love to have coffee with you and hear all about it," Edna murmured, tongue in cheek.

"Everything I know is classified," Lang said. "But I can sure tell you about weapons technology."

"Oh, we learned all about that by watching the latest *Lethal Weapon* movie," Edna informed him.

"Not quite." He glanced at the dilapidated coffee machine. "First thing we're going to do is replace that."

Edna spread-eagled her thin frame in front of it. "Over my dead body!" she exclaimed. "If it goes, I go."

Lang peered down at her. "Makes good coffee, does it?"

"The best," she assured him.

"Prove it," he challenged.

Her dark eyes sparkled. "My pleasure," she said, and proceeded to crank up the veteran machine.

Ten minutes later, Lang had to agree that they couldn't take a chance on a new coffeemaker being up to those standards. His co-workers chuckled, and decided that the new addition might not be such a pain, after all.

The next day, dressed in his best gray suit, red-striped tie and neatly pressed cotton shirt, Lang made a tour of the five companies under the Lancaster, Incorporated umbrella.

The first was Lancaster, Inc., itself, which owned and was located in a huge office complex that served as headquarters for several other San Antonio companies. There were ten security people, five day and five night, who looked after the safety of the various buildings. One did nothing but assure the safety of the parking garage adjacent to it, and inspected the parking permits of the complex's occupants. The others patrolled in cars and on foot, maintaining a high level of security.

He interviewed the personnel and found one particular man not at all to his liking. There was something about the security officer that disturbed him, more so when Lang caught him calling out a very personal remark to one of the women who worked in the building. Perhaps they were friends, because the woman smiled wanly and kept walking. But Lang remembered the incident later, when he was talking to the building's main security officer.

Two of the headquarters' offices located in this complex—one a canning concern and the other a meat packer—had been targeted by protestors from various radical groups, Lang was told by the main security officer, a man younger than Lang. Security was responsible for seeing to it that none of the tenants got hurt. Lang asked casually if the man had any problems with his personnel. There was a pregnant pause, and he told Lang that he'd had a complaint or two about one of the men, but he was keeping a close eye on him. Lang didn't like the sound of that.

Lang's second charge was a department store of vintage age, where two stories of fine clothing were under the care of two day-security people and one night guard. The younger of the three was a little cocky until he learned Lang's background, and then it was amusing to watch him backpedal and try to make amends.

The third of the businesses was a small garment company that manufactured blue jeans. It had only one security guard for day and one for night. Lang liked the night man, who was a veteran of the Drug Enforcement Administration. He'd have to make a point of stopping by one night to talk over old times with him.

The fourth company was a licensed warehouse where imported goods were brought and stored until they cleared customs.

And the fifth company under the umbrella of Lancaster, Inc.'s, security network was a new and thriving company called Contacts Unlimited. It boasted six executives and ten employees in the Lancaster, Inc., office complex where Lang had started out investigating his security force that morning.

Lang spoke to the company president, Mack Dunlap, about any complaints he might have with the company's security. It was a follow-up to the talk he'd already had with the complex's main security official, who was under Lang's authority now.

"Not me," Mack, a tall balding man, said brightly. "But one of our vice presidents says that one of the day-security men made a very suggestive remark to her."

Lang's eyes narrowed. "Did he, now?" he asked. "I'd like a word with her. Naturally I'm going to take such complaints very seriously."

Mack's eyebrows went up. "That's new. Old Baxter, who had the job before you, just laughed. He said women should get used to that sort of talk. She had words with him, let me tell you."

"I can't do anything about Baxter, but I can promise you that a new yardstick will be used to measure our security people from now on."

Mack smiled. "Thanks. Uh, right down there, second door to the left. She's in this afternoon."

"I'll only take a minute of her time," Lang said with formal politeness.

He went to the door, not really noticing the nameplate, and knocked.

"Come in," came a poised, quietly feminine voice.

He opened the door and froze in the doorway.

She was dressed in an off-white linen suit with a pea green blouse that just matched her eyes. Her blond hair was cut short around her face, curling toward high cheekbones and a bow-shaped mouth.

She was looking down at a spreadsheet, her thin eyebrows drawn into a slight frown as she tried to unravel some figures that had her puzzled.

"What can I do for you, Mack?" she asked absently, without looking up.

Lang's hand tightened on the doorknob. All the memories were rushing back at him from out of the past, stinging his heart, his mind, making him hoarse. Bob's grinning face flashed in his mind, and now he knew why his brother had reacted so strongly to news that Lang was going to work for Lancaster, Inc.

"I said..." Kirry looked up, and those green eyes went from shock to fascination to sheer hatred in a split second. She stood up, as slender and pretty as ever, but with a new maturity about her.

"Hello, Kirry," Lang said quietly, forcing himself to smile with careless indifference. "Long time no see."

"What is the CIA doing here?" she wanted to know.

Lang looked around. "What CIA?"

"You!"

"Oh. I'm not CIA. Well, not anymore," he replied. "I just went to work for Lancaster, Inc. I'm their new chief of security." He grinned from ear to ear at her discomfort. "Isn't it a small world!"

Two

Kirry sat back down, as gracefully as she could with her heart breaking inside her body. She forced a smile, almost as careless as Lang's.

"Yes," she said, "it is a small world. What can I do for you, Lang?"

"Your boss says you've had some problems with one of our security people."

"Oh."

He stuck his hands into his pockets. "Well?"

So he hadn't found out where she worked and come just to see her. It was business. That shouldn't have disappointed her. After all, it was five years ago when he stormed out of her life. But it did disappoint her.

He wasn't smoking. In the old days, there had always been a cigarette dangling from his fingers. She wondered why he'd given it up. Perhaps they didn't let secret agents smoke or practice any other addictions that might put the job at risk.

"Mr. Erikson seems to find it amusing to make vulgar remarks to me," she said, easing down into her chair with assumed nonchalance.

"Tell Mr. Erikson to cut it out."

"I have. He can't understand why I should find it offensive. I am a woman, after all. Women were created, or so he says, for man's pleasure," she added meaningfully.

He pursed his lips. "I see. How old a man are we discussing?"

"He's somewhere near fifty, I guess."

"He should know better."

"I hope you'll make that clear. I came very close to filing charges against him yesterday."

"For what?"

She didn't like discussing it with Lang. She hesitated.

"We were friends once," he reminded her.

"He was making remarks about the size of my foundation garments and whether or not I wore black ones. Then he proceeded to say," she said, taking a breath, "that he'd buy me one if I'd put it on for him."

Lang didn't like that, and it showed. "I'll have to have a little talk with him. If it happens again, I want to know."

She met his eyes levelly. "If it does, I'll have him prosecuted. Nobody should have to take that kind of abuse just to hold down a job. This is a good job, too. I don't want to lose it."

"You won't." He turned back toward the door, his hand on the knob, and looked back at her quietly. "How's your mother?" he asked.

"I have no idea," she replied coolly. "The last I heard, she and her fourth husband were living in Denmark."

He averted his eyes and left without a conventional goodbye.

Kirry unclasped her hands and discovered that they were cold and shaking. It had been a long time since she'd let her nerves affect her like this. Even finals every semester at college hadn't rattled her this badly. Of course, Lang was much worse than tests.

She tried to concentrate on her work, but her mind kept returning to the turbulent days before Lang had left town. She made a cursory examination of a new file, but she couldn't keep her mind on it.

She turned her swivel chair around and looked out the window. Lang had just left the building. He was getting into a late-model car with Lancaster, Inc., Security written on the side of it. His dark hair had the sheen of a raven's wing in the sun. She remembered how it had felt to touch it, to let it ripple through her fingers in the darkness of a parked car. So many years ago. . . .

The buzzer distracted her. She picked up the receiver. "Yes?"

"It's me, Kirry. Betty," her friend said, identifying herself. "You really get results, don't you?" She laughed.

"What do you mean?"

"Our friend Erikson just got the boot. He mouthed off at Daddy Lancaster's new security chief about women being fair game for any man. His jaw is still dangling."

Kirry caught her breath. "Lang fired him!"

"Lang?"

"Lang Patton. The new security chief. I . . . used to know him, when I was younger."

"Ah, so that's how the wind blows."

"You didn't think I was going to take it much longer?" she asked.

"No. And I wasn't, either. All of us were sick of Erikson's innuendos. We're going to take you out to lunch. Just think, maybe Mr. Patton will send us somebody young and handsome and single."

"He'll probably send you an ex-marine with a sweet tooth." Kirry chuckled.

"Spoilsport. Listen, Erikson's pretty mad. You should steer clear of this area until he leaves."

"I'm not afraid of him."

"Well, you might be wise to avoid him, just the same. See you later."

Betty hung up and Kirry bit her lower lip. She hadn't wanted to cause trouble. Most men were polite and courteous. But Erickson had been menacing with his remarks and the way he looked at women. Kirry felt unclean when she had to pass him in the hall.

At first she'd thought that perhaps she was overreacting. After all, she'd just come from university, where men and women enjoyed an intellectual kinship that usually precluded sexist remarks on either side. But in the real world there were men still mentally living in an age when women were treated as sexual property. It had come as a shock to Kirry to find herself working in the same close area with a man who felt free to make suggestive remarks to any woman he chose.

Erikson had actually pinched Betty on the buttocks, and when she'd slapped him, he'd laughed and said wasn't that cute. Women always meant yes, even when they said no, he added.

Kirry could have told Lang a lot more than she had, but apparently he'd found out Erikson for himself. She felt both relieved and sick at the firing. Erikson had no family, but he was an older man and he might have a hard time finding another job. For that, she felt guilty. Even knowing that the man had brought it on himself didn't make her feel a lot better.

The phone rang and Kirry picked it up.

"Don't think you're going to get away with it, telling all those lies about me," Erikson's harsh voice informed her. "I'll get you. Count on it."

The receiver went down and Kirry felt a curl of real fear. Surely it was just bad temper. He'd get over it. But in the meantime, she was going to make sure that she never presented him with any opportunities to make his threat known. And perhaps she should mention it to Lang. Just in case.

That evening when she went home, she made sure that she left in broad daylight. There would be no more working late, she told her boss, until the threat was over, and Mack had agreed wholeheartedly.

It was a long walk from the parking lot into her apartment building. She looked around, but she didn't see anything out of the ordinary. She went inside, grateful that there was a security man even here, and quickly went up to her apartment on the second floor.

She'd decorated it with a lot of greenery and simple furniture. It was a lonely apartment, but very pretty, and she had her own little kitchenette. Not only that, there was a balcony. The balcony had been the drawing card when she settled here. It overlooked the Alamo in the distance, and she had a mesquite tree just outside it, with long feathery fronds of greenery trailing to the ground. She loved the tree and the view. She had a lounge chair out there, so she could laze in the spring sunlight.

After she changed into jeans and a loose knit blouse, she fixed herself a cup of coffee and slid onto the lounger. The sun, late afternoon though it was, felt good on her face.

She remembered another spring afternoon, the day she'd realized that she was falling in love with Lang

Patton. She'd been lazing away in the tree in her front yard in Floresville. She'd been just sixteen years old. The Campbell house in those days was just down the street from the Patton home place. Lang was out of school by then and working with the San Antonio police force, but he came home on weekends sometimes to visit his parents and his brother. He'd been going with a model named Lorna McLane, but they'd just broken up. He was alone now when he came home. Kirry was glad. She didn't like the superior way Lorna looked down her nose at people.

Kirry had always known Lang. He'd been like a big brother to her most of her life.

"Get down out of there before you kill yourself," he'd called up to her, grinning as he stood below in a black T-shirt and blue jeans. He was powerfully built and she loved to look at him. It made her tingle all over.

"It isn't against the law to climb trees," she informed him pertly, laughing. "Go arrest somebody else."

"I'm very happy where I am, thanks." He looked for footholds and handholds, and a minute later he was up in the next limb, leaning back against the big oak's trunk. "Here. Have a pear." He produced one from his pocket and retrieved his own from the other.

Lang had noticed her, too, that day. His eyes had been slow and bold on her long, tanned legs and the thrust of her breasts in the front-tied blouse she was wearing with her cutoffs. He hadn't made a move in her direction. But after that day, he'd teased her and their relationship had turned to friendship.

How long ago it seemed that Lang had made time to listen to her problems at school. Her mother was too busy getting married and divorced to pay Kirry much attention, and she had no other relatives. She gravitated toward the Patton place. Lang's mother had been dead for years. Nobody ever talked about her, least of all Lang. When Lang's father died suddenly of a heart attack, Kirry was there with quiet sympathy and compassion. She sat and held Lang's hand all during the funeral. When Bob and Connie's son Mikey had been born, Kirry had gone with Lang to the christening. And all at once, Lang was everywhere she went....

The ringing of the telephone made her jump. She went to answer it and hesitated uncharacteristically. Surely it wouldn't be Erikson. Would it?

Her heart was pounding as she lifted the receiver.

"Kirry?"

It was Lang. She relaxed, but only a little. "Hi, Lang."

"I thought you should know that I fired Erikson this afternoon," he said quietly. "He was pretty mad. If he gives you any trouble, I want to know about it."

"He called me before he left," she returned. "He said he was going to 'get me.'"

There was a pause. "Did that frighten you?"

She smiled, and twirled the phone cord around her fingers. "A little."

"Really?" There was a smile in his voice. "The girl I used to know would have laid his head open with a baseball bat."

"My mother never cared about me enough to fight my battles. I had to grow up tough."

"I fought some of them for you," he reminded her.

"Oh, yes. You were my friend." The eyes he couldn't see were sad, full of bad memories. "I have to go, Lang."

"Wait."

"We have nothing to say," she replied sadly.

"I'm sorry you wouldn't read the letter I sent you, Kirry," he said after a minute.

"You didn't trust me," she reminded him. "You thought that I was a two-timing playgirl."

"I was crazy with jealousy," he replied. "Didn't you know that I'd cool down and come to my senses eventually?"

She laughed bitterly. "By the time you did, I'd stopped caring. I was dating a new guy at college and enjoying myself," she lied with finesse. Not for worlds would she tell him how it had really been when he refused to listen to her explanations.

Lang froze inside. He'd thought Kirry loved him. If she'd taken up with someone else so quickly, she couldn't have. It was an unexpected blow to his ego. "Then it was just as well that you refused to accept it."

"Was there anything else?" she asked politely.

"Yes. Let me know if you have any more contact with Erikson," he replied. "He's mixed up with a couple of the local outer-fringe elements. I think he's loopy."

"Nice word."

"Do you think so?" he said, grinning. "I'm thinking of buying the rights to it."

"I'll call you if I have any trouble. Thanks for checking, Lang."

"Sure."

She put down the receiver, idly caressing it as she thought about how it had felt to kiss Lang. Pipe dreams, she reminded herself. She couldn't afford to go that route again. It had really broken her up to lose him, especially since her mother had been in the throes of another divorce at the time. Her home life had been virtually nonexistent, and that was one reason she'd gone off to university without a protest. It seemed like a lifetime ago now. She had to make sure that it stayed that way.

Lang settled in at his hotel and went to work. Within a week he had a grasp on the security setup within the Lancaster organization, and he was confident that he could upgrade it to a more efficient level.

Kirry worried him, though. She'd been very cautious in her movements for a few days after Erikson was fired, but she'd suddenly grown careless. Today she was working late, and it was already dark. Lang knew for a fact that her parking lot would be deserted. He decided that in the interest of keeping her safe, he'd better check on her.

Sure enough, the parking lot *was* deserted, except for an older-model blue sedan with a familiar face in it.

Confrontation, Lang had found, was the best way to avoid real trouble. He pulled up beside the blue sedan and got out of his security car. He was wearing an automatic under his arm, a necessity in his new line of work. He hoped he wouldn't have to pull it.

"What are you doing here, Erikson?" Lang asked. "You're on private property."

Erikson, a thin, cold-eyed man, looked vaguely disconcerted by Lang's direct approach. "I'm enjoying the view."

"Enjoy it from another perspective," Lang suggested to him with a dangerous smile. "And in case you have any ideas about retribution, you'd do better to forget them. You may have had a few years experience in the army and as a security guard, but I was CIA for five years. I've forgotten tricks you never even learned."

The implied threat seemed to be enough. Without a reply, Erikson started his car and pulled out of the parking lot, giving Lang a resentful glare on the way.

Lang watched him drive out of sight before he turned and went into the building.

Kirry was at her desk, talking on the phone to someone who was obviously a client.

"You have nothing to worry about!" she was reassuring the party at the end of the line. "Honestly, it's all under control. That's right. We'll take care of everything. All you have to do is just show up, okay?

Okay. We'll take good care of you. Yes. Yes. Certainly. Thank *you!* Goodbye.''

She hung up with an audible sigh of relief and leaned back in her chair. Her green eyes found Lang in the doorway and she jumped, but not with fear. The impact of his presence had always caused that reaction, although she was usually able to hide it. Tonight, she was tired. Ten things had gone wrong since she walked in the door, and she'd spent the day untying tangles.

"I didn't think anyone was still in the building," she said, sitting up.

"I came by to check the parking lot," he said, shrugging his big shoulders. The soft fabric of his gray-and-tan sport coat moved with the action, and the bulge under his arm was visible.

"You're wearing a gun," she accused involuntarily.

His expression was unfamiliar as he looked at her. "I've worn a gun for a long time. You never used to pay any attention to it."

"That was before you signed on with the Company and went off to see how many bullets you could collect and still live," she said with a sweet smile that didn't reach her eyes.

"Don't tell me you cared, cupcake."

She lowered her eyes. She was wearing a neat gray suit with a pale pink knit blouse, and she looked fragile and very pretty. Lang couldn't drag his eyes away from her.

"I thought I did," she replied. "But you cured me."

He moved forward, cleared a corner of her cluttered desk and perched himself there. The movement pulled his slacks taut across his powerful thighs. Kirry had to fight not to look at them. She'd touched him there, once. She could still remember the impact of it, his hand guiding hers in the heat of passion, his hoarse moan when she began to caress him....

"Why are you still here?" he asked, breaking into her embarrassing thoughts.

"Business," she said, clearing her throat. "I'm a vice president. I'm in charge of arrangements when we have our clients make personal appearances. Sometimes things go wrong, like today."

"And you have to clean them up."

She smiled. "That's right."

"It's dark outside."

"Yes, I know. I have this, though." She produced a key chain with a small container of Mace.

He sighed gently. "Kirry, what if the wind's in the wrong direction when you use it? And do you realize how close you have to be?"

She flushed. "Well, I have this, too." She held up a canned "screamer."

"Great. What if there's nobody within hearing range?"

She began to feel nervous. If there was one thing Lang did know about, it was personal protection. "I don't like guns," she began.

"A gun is the last thing you need. Have you taken any self-defense courses at all?"

"No. I don't have time."

"Make time," he said bluntly.

He looked concerned. That disturbed her. She began to make connections. His presence here, his insistence on protection for her...

"Somebody was in the parking lot," she said astutely, her green eyes narrowed and intent on his hard face. "Erikson?"

He nodded. "I threatened him and ran him out of the parking lot. But I can't run him off a public street, you understand? There's no law against it."

"But that's called stalking," she said uneasily.

"And right now, it isn't against the law," he replied grimly.

She recalled cases she'd seen on television, mostly of angry ex-boyfriends or ex-husbands who stalked and finally killed women. The police could do nothing because a crime had to be committed before the police could act. And by the time that happened, usually it was too late for the victim.

"He wouldn't kill me," she stammered.

"There are other things he could do," Lang said distastefully.

Her lips parted as she let out a quick breath. "I don't believe this," she said. "I was only defending myself against an impossible situation. I never meant..."

"Do you think it would have gotten better if you'd ignored it?" he asked gently. "Men like that don't stop. They get worse. You know that."

She pushed back her wavy blond hair. "I know, but I never expected this." Her wide eyes sought his. "He'll quit, won't he? He'll get tired of it and go away?"

He picked up a paper clip on her desk and twisted it between his long, broad fingers. "I don't think so."

Her hands felt cold. She clasped them together, with a sick feeling in the pit of her stomach making her uncomfortable. "What can I do?"

"I'll try to keep an eye on you as much as I can," he began.

"Lang, that won't do," she said. "You can't watch me all the time. It wouldn't be fair to ask you to. I have to be able to take care of myself." She looked down at her slender body, remembering that Erikson was much taller and outweighed her by about sixty pounds. She smiled ruefully. "I can't believe I'll ever frighten anyone with self-defense, but I guess I'll see if I can find a class to join."

"Most of them are at night," he said. "Very few karate instructors can afford to operate a martial arts studio full-time."

"Surely there are Saturday classes," she said.

"Maybe." He smiled tenderly. "But nobody can teach you self-defense better than I can. And I can keep an eye on you in the process."

She averted her eyes. "That wouldn't be a good idea."

He studied her down-bent head with faint guilt. "We were friends once. More than friends," he reminded her softly. "Can't you pretend that nothing happened between us, just for a few weeks, until we can solve the problem of Erikson?''

Her eyes were wary, distrustful. "I don't know, Lang."

"We're different people," he said, pointedly. "If I'm not, why would I have left the Company?"

She frowned. "I hadn't thought about that. Why did you leave it? Even when you were younger, all you talked about was becoming an agent."

"I got my priorities straight," he returned.

"Did you really?" Her eyes narrowed. "How did you know that Lancaster, Inc., needed a new security chief?"

"A friend told me," he said. He wasn't going to tell her who the friend was. Not yet. She'd never liked Lorna, and the reverse was also true. Lorna didn't have any romantic designs on him, but he didn't want Kirry to know. Not yet.

His dark eyes slid over her face, down to her slender body and back up again. He wanted so badly to ask if there was a man in her life, but that was too much too soon. Besides, he had to be sure about his own feelings before he started trying to coax hers. He couldn't bear to hurt her again.

"I don't know if I'd be any good at martial arts," she began slowly.

She was going to give in. He knew it instinctively, and it delighted him. He smiled at her without mockery or malice. "Let's find out," he suggested.

Her breath sighed out. "All right. I'll have to fit it in with work, though. When?"

"Two nights a week, two hours a night," he said. "And you'll have to practice at home, too."

"This sounds like a lot of work," she mumbled.

"It is. But it's worth it. It could save your life."

"You're really concerned about Erikson, aren't you?" she asked. If Lang was worried, there was a cause for concern.

"Let's say that I'm staying on the right side of caution," he corrected. His big shoulders lifted and fell carelessly, and he smiled at her. "Humor me. For old times' sake."

She frowned and chewed on a fingernail while she pondered the anguish of being so close to Lang when she'd spent years trying to forget him.

"Or am I overlooking the obvious?" he asked suddenly, and his face changed, hardened. "Is there a man in the picture, someone who expects your company in the evenings?"

She wished with all her heart that she could answer him in the affirmative. Ridiculous, to pine for a man all that time, and after he'd treated her so shabbily. But he did look different. He wasn't the same hard-nosed, arrogant man who'd left Floresville to join the Company several years ago. He'd mellowed. The threat was still there, the ruthlessness, but there was a new tenderness, too.

"No, Lang," she said. "There's no one."

His eyelids flickered, but his face gave away nothing. "All right, then. Suppose we go shopping tomorrow when you get off work, and we'll begin tomorrow night?"

She frowned. "Shopping? For what?"

He chuckled. "Wait and see."

Three

▬

Kirry groaned as she looked at herself in the mirror. "Lang, it looks like pajamas," she moaned.

Lang opened the door to her bedroom and leaned against the doorjamb, his arms folded, to study her. She was wearing what they'd bought that afternoon; it was a white gi, the traditional karate uniform of white pants and a white top with one side folded over the other. For a beginner, the first gi was secured by a white belt. Colored belts had to be earned with new skills at each level of accomplishment, the highest of which was black.

Kirry looked fragile in the outfit, slender and not at all threatening. Her head was bent, her shoulders slumped, baring her nape where her hair was short in back.

"Let me explain something to you," he said disapprovingly, jerking away from the doorframe to stand just behind her. "The first rule of self-defense is to never look vulnerable. In the wild, an animal will never show illness, right up to the point of death, to prevent being attacked. It isn't much different with people. A potential attacker can spot an easy victim."

"How?" she asked, peering into his eyes in the mirror.

"You carry yourself as if you've already been beaten, didn't you know?" he asked gently. "Your shoulders are thrown forward. You keep your eyes and head down when you walk. You clutch your bag close—not a bad idea, but the way you do it is a dead giveaway."

"What should I do, walk down the street aiming karate chops at every tree I pass?" she asked.

He grinned. "Not a bad idea, if you can learn how to knock one down that way. Otherwise, pass on it. Listen, you have to walk as if you own the world and know full well that you can break every bone in an attacker's body. Sometimes just your posture is enough to ward off trouble. Stand up straight."

She did, giving her slender body an added elegance.

"Now hold your head up. Don't make long eye contact—a man might construe that as an invitation—but don't keep your eyes down as if you're afraid to look at people."

"I am, sometimes," she confessed with a faint smile. "People intimidate me."

"Right. That's why you're in a public relations job."

"I can bluff enough to do my job. It's after work that gives me problems," she said with a sigh, glancing critically at herself in the mirror. "I don't mix well."

"You always were shy, except with people you knew," he recalled. His eyes dropped to her soft mouth, pink with lipstick, and he remembered it clinging hotly to him, pleading for more than any honorable man could give her. He hadn't wanted to get married, and Kirry was not the sort of girl he felt comfortable seducing outside of marriage. He'd talked about marrying her, and he knew that it was what she wanted, but things hadn't worked out. It had been a sad situation altogether, and he still wasn't proud of his solution. Instead of just telling her he didn't want to get married, he'd made a run for it. And his best friend had unwittingly given him the escape he needed. Kirry had been the one who'd suffered the most.

"Would you mind not looking at me like that?" she asked, lifting her green eyes to his dark ones in the mirror. "This is nice of you, to teach me how to take care of myself, but I'd rather if it wasn't... uncomfortable."

"Sorry," he said abruptly. "Back to what I was telling you," he said, changing the subject. "Walk with a purpose when you go out, as if you know exactly where you're going—even if you're lost. Keep your chin up, look at people, but just enough to let them know you see them. When you're going to your car, always have your keys in your hand, not in your purse. Look in the back seat and all around before you open the door and get in, and then lock it. Don't ever go into a dark parking lot alone at night, or to an automated bank teller. Women have risked that and turned up dead.''

She shivered. ''You're frightening me.''

''I want to,'' he said. His dark eyes didn't blink. ''I want you to understand how drastic the consequences can be.''

''Women should be able to go wherever they like....''

''Don't hand me that,'' he said shortly. ''So should men and kids, but they must abide by the same rules. It's that sort of world. Nobody is safe in a city alone after dark, man, woman or child. Men get attacked, too, you know, even if it isn't usually for the same reasons that women do.''

''Our culture is sick,'' she remarked philosophically.

''Whatever. We deal with it as best we can. What I'm going to teach you will keep you alive, at least. Come on. Get your coat.''

''But I thought we were going to practice here....'' she began.

''Do you really like the idea of being thrown flat on your back on a wood floor?'' he asked pleasantly.

She glowered at him. ''What do you mean, thrown on my back?''

"Didn't I mention it? In karate, the first thing they teach you is how to fall correctly. You're going to be falling a lot, flat on your back and every other way."

"You're kidding!"

"Think so?" He handed her the lightweight car coat she wore on cool spring nights.

She put it on with a resigned breath. She hoped she could work with broken bones.

Lang had a friend who ran a gym. The man was middle-aged, but very muscular and fit, and he and Lang seemed to know each other from way back.

"Karate, huh?" the man, Tony, mused, studying Kirry. "Is she tough enough?"

Kirry drew herself to her full height and glared at him. "She sure is," she said with a jerk of her head.

He chuckled. "Good. If Lang teaches you, you'll need to be. Most of his students quit after the first night when he was on the police force, teaching it in his spare time."

Tony ambled away and Kirry followed Lang over to a long, thick mat on the floor of the gym near the wall. "I didn't know you taught karate," she remarked.

"You didn't know a lot of things that I did," he replied carelessly. "You know how to stretch, don't you?"

"Yes. I do that every morning."

"Do some stretches while I get into my gi."

He walked away with his black duffel bag, and Kirry settled onto the mat.

While the minutes ticked away, she became slowly aware of curious glances from some of the other occupants of the gym. Most of them were working out on machines. Two young women were lifting weights. Another was doing isometric exercises.

Loud noises from the other end of the gym drew her attention. She noticed several men gathered around a punching bag near where Lang had gone. Someone was doing kicks and spins with incredible speed and grace, which made Kirry dizzy. She paused in her own stretching just to watch him. He went up with a high jump kick and the gym vibrated as his foot connected with the hanging bag. He landed and turned, laughing, and she suddenly recognized him. It was Lang!

She stared at him as he spoke to the men and walked toward her. The gi fit him very nicely, loose though it was, giving an impression of great strength. Her eyes fell to his belt and she wasn't surprised to see that it was black, the hallmark of the highest ranks of skill in the sport.

"We'd better stop right now," she told him breathlessly, "because I'm never going to be able to do what you just did."

He grinned. "Not today, anyway. Limbered up, are we?"

She grimaced. "I guess." She eyed him warily. "Did you mean it, about making me fall?"

He nodded. "Don't worry. There's a right way to do it. You won't get hurt."

That was what he thought. Just being close to him made all her senses stir.

"Ready to get started?" he asked. His eyes fell to her watch. "Take that off," he said. "Never wear jewelry on the mat, it's dangerous."

"Oh. Sorry." She stripped it off and slipped it into the pocket of her coat. There were no rings to worry about. She hadn't worn a ring since Lang had given her a small emerald one for her birthday. She still had it, safe in a drawer, but she never put it on.

She went back to the mat. He taught her how to approach the mat, because there was ritual and reverence even in that. Then he taught her the bow to an opponent. Afterward, he taught her the rigorous disciplined stretches that preceded all karate lessons. She was worn-out from them before he took her back to the mat and showed her how to do left and right side break falls and back break falls. She spent the next hour falling down. Once she missed the mat and landed on her hip on the hard gym floor.

"You said it wouldn't hurt," she muttered, rubbing her behind.

"It doesn't, if you land where you're supposed to," he returned. "Watch where you're going."

"Yes, sir," she murmured with a mischievous glance.

"Fall down."

She groaned. "Which way?"

"Your choice."

"My choice would be a nice hot bath and bed," she told him.

He smiled. "Tired?"

She hesitated, then she nodded.

"Okay, tiger, that's enough for today. Attention." He called her to the beginning stance. "Bow."

She bowed. He left her to change back into his street clothes and she leaned against the wall, feeling pummeled.

They drove home in a contented silence.

"What kind of karate is it?" she asked. "During that last break one of the men mentioned that there are different kinds."

"You're studying tae kwon do," he told her. "It's a Korean form of martial art, one which specializes in kicks."

"Kicks."

"You've got the legs for it, and I don't mean that in an offensive way," he added. "You have long legs, and they're strong ones. Kicks are potentially much more dangerous than hand blows."

"I felt the gym shake when you did that jump kick, just after you put on your gi," she murmured demurely.

He chuckled. "I did nothing but practice when I first joined the police force. While the other single guys were out chasing women and drinking beer in their spare time, I was in the gym learning how to do spin kicks."

"You're . . . amazing to watch," she said, searching for the right word to describe the elegant skill of his movements.

He smiled. "Flattery?"

"Not at all!"

"If you work at it, you can do those same moves," he said. "Plenty of women are black belts. In fact, I worked on a case with another Company agent who had a higher rank than mine. She taught me some new moves."

She closed up. "Did she?" she asked, glancing out the window.

He smiled to himself. The woman he'd just mentioned was a retired army officer of sixty. He wouldn't disillusion Kirry by passing that little bit of information along.

"Want to stop somewhere for a cup of coffee?" he asked.

"I can't drink it at night," she said apologetically. "I like to be in bed by ten."

He scowled. "Woman, what kind of life are you living!"

Not much of one, she could have said. "Oh, I stay up if there's a good movie on," she said defensively.

"You're twenty-two."

"Twenty-three," she corrected.

"Twenty-three, then," he returned. "You're too young to spend that much time alone."

"I didn't say I was always alone," she said stiffly. "I go out on dates!" And she did. The last one had been a newly divorced man who talked about his ex-wife and cried. The one before that was a bachelor of fifty who wanted her to move in with him. She hadn't had a lot of luck in her search for companionship, least of all with Lang, whose memory had stood between her and the most innocent involvement with anyone else.

Lang didn't know the true circumstances, though. He was picturing Kirry in another man's arms, and he didn't like it. His hands tightened on the steering wheel.

"You used to smoke," she remarked.

"Only occasionally," he replied. "It was interfering with my wind when I worked out, so I gave it up."

"Good for you," she murmured.

He pulled into the parking lot of her apartment building. A car pulled in behind them. A blue sedan.

Lang saw it and suddenly spun his own car around and headed straight for it. He didn't look as if he meant to stop, and the one glimpse Kirry got of his face made her cling to the seat for all she was worth.

Apparently the ruthless maneuver got the message across to Erikson in the blue sedan, because he burned rubber getting out of the parking lot and down the street.

"Damn him," Lang said icily when he'd parked the car. "Maybe I should just beat the hell out of him and put him in the hospital for a few weeks. That might get the idea across."

Kirry was unnerved. She looked at Lang warily. "No," she said. "You mustn't do that. He'd have you put in jail."

"He'd have a hard time keeping me there," he returned with a smile. "I have connections."

She twisted her small clutch bag in her hands. "I thought I was doing the right thing, telling you about him...."

"You did," he replied. "The days of men like Erikson are over. It's just going to take a few lawsuits to convince them of it."

"Stalkers kill people," she said, voicing her worst fear.

"Erikson won't kill you," he replied. "And after I've worked out with you for a few weeks, he'll regret it if he comes within striking range."

She smiled. "Think so? What am I going to do, fall on him?"

"You're pretty good at that," he said with an instructor's pride in his student.

"Thanks."

"I'll walk you up, just in case."

He got out of the car, locked it and came around to take her soft hand in his as they went into the building and stood waiting for the elevator.

Kirry should have pulled her hand away, but she couldn't manage. It brought back memories of their first real date. He'd held her hand then, too, and she could still feel the thrill of it.

"It was your first date, and you were so nervous that you were trembling when I took you home that night," he recalled, glancing down at her surprised face. "Am I reading your mind again?" he asked, lifting their clasped hands. "You aren't the only one with memories. They aren't all bad ones, are they?"

She didn't answer him. The elevator door opened and they stepped into the deserted conveyance. Lang pushed the button for her floor.

"We could have walked up, it's just the second floor," she reminded him.

"Stay out of stairwells," he replied seriously.

"Oh. Yes, I see."

"That goes for work as well as home," he added.

The elevator door opened and he walked her down to the end of the deserted corridor, where her apartment was. He noticed that she had her key in her hand when they got there. No fumbling for it in a purse or pocket. He smiled.

"Kirry?" he asked as she unlocked the door.

She hesitated, with her back to him.

"Do you want the conventional end to the evening?" he asked quietly.

Her hand clenched on the doorknob as she remembered how it felt to kiss him. "It wouldn't be wise."

"Probably not." He shoved his hands into his pockets and leaned his shoulder against the wall next to the door. His dark eyes slid over her profile. "What ever happened to Chad?" he asked.

Her eyes shot to his. "Don't you know? He was your best friend."

"Not after he broke us up," he replied tightly. "Or didn't anyone ever tell you that I knocked two of his teeth out?"

"No," she said. She huddled closer into her jacket, chilled by the look on Lang's face. "It was a little late, though, wasn't it?"

"Made me feel better," he said laconically.

His broad chest rose and fell under the soft knit shirt he was wearing. There was a dark shadow under it. He was hairy under his shirt. Kirry had delighted in burying her hands and her mouth in that soft thicket.

The sadness she felt was reflected in the eyes she lifted to his broad face. "You never really knew anything about me," she said suddenly, "except that you liked to kiss me." She smiled gently. "Maybe that's why you wouldn't listen when I told you that Chad had framed me."

He didn't answer her. His eyes fell to her mouth and lingered there until she moved restlessly and her hand turned on the doorknob.

"The first time I kissed you, you gasped under my mouth," he recalled quietly. "It surprised me that you didn't know what a deep kiss felt like."

She felt uncomfortable. Her green eyes glittered at him angrily. "There's no need to rub it in."

"If you hadn't been a virgin, our lives would have been a lot different," he continued. "I wanted you so badly that I couldn't think straight, but you were the original old-fashioned girl. No sex before marriage."

"I'm still the original old-fashioned woman," she told him proudly. "My body is my business. I can do whatever I want to with it, and that includes being celibate if I feel like it."

"Nights must get real cold in winter," he chided.

Her eyebrows lifted. "I have an electric blanket, dear man, and no health worries. I sleep like a top. How about you?"

He didn't sleep well. He hadn't for years. His memories were of the violent variety and in the past few months, they'd become constant and nightmarish.

"I don't," he replied frankly.

"No wonder," she returned. "All those women!"

"Kirry..."

He couldn't deny it, of course he couldn't. She fought down the jealousy and smiled. "Thanks for the lesson."

He clamped down hard on his temper. "No problem," he replied after a minute. "We'll do it again in three days. Remember those stretches. Practice them."

Her mind darted back to Erikson in the parking lot, and she felt threatened. Her eyes showed it.

"Don't let him see that he's scared you," Lang said curtly. "Don't you dare let him know. Keep your chin up. Look at him, show him you aren't intimidated. Make sure you're with people when you leave the building, here or at work."

"Okay."

He smiled softly. "You're tough. Remember it."

"I'll try. Thanks, Lang."

"I'll be around. Let me know if you need me."

She nodded.

He pushed away from the wall and looked down at her almost hungrily before he turned and walked slowly back toward the elevator.

Kirry wanted to call him back. She knew the sight of that retreating back, because she'd lived with it all these years. It still hurt to watch him go. Nothing had changed at all.

When he got to the elevator and pressed the button he turned and caught her staring at him. He looked back, aching to hold her. He had a feeling that he was going to get postgraduate courses in self-denial before this Erikson business was through.

Kirry lifted her hand in a halfhearted wave and went into her apartment, closing the door and locking it behind her. She had to stop wanting Lang to kiss her. It would be the same old mess again if she encouraged him. This time, she was going to be strong.

That attitude lasted all night long. It got her to work and into the building, despite the sight of that damned blue sedan sitting on the street in front of her apartment building and following her all the way to Lancaster, Inc. She looked straight at Erikson without a smile or a flinch as she went into the building, and it seemed to disconcert him. Lang had been right, she thought as she went into her office. It really was working! She felt better than she had since the ordeal had begun.

Kirry was promoting a public seminar for a local business firm that specialized in interior design. She'd arranged for a special appearance by a famed European designer at one of San Antonio's biggest malls, and coordinated it with an amateur competition for local citizens who'd done their own decorating. The European designer was to judge the entries and Kirry had bought advertising on local television stations and newspapers, all of which had promised to send reporters to cover the event.

It was time-consuming and maddening to get all the details to fit together, though, and by the time Kirry had them finalized, she was a nervous wreck.

It didn't help that when she went out to her car that infernal blue sedan was sitting there like a land shark, with Erikson in the front seat glaring at her.

Furious, she went back into the building and called the police. She explained the problem to a sympathetic officer on the desk.

"Is his car in the parking lot of your business, Miss Campbell?" he asked politely.

"Well, no. It's on the street across from the parking lot."

"A public street?"

She grimaced. "Yes."

There was a pause. "I don't like saying this, but I have to. There's no law against a man sitting in his car, no matter what threats he might have made. If he hasn't actually assaulted you, or said anything to you, there isn't a single thing we can do."

"But he's stalking me," she groaned.

"The law needs to be changed," he told her. "And it will be. But right now, the law says that we can't touch him. On the other hand, if he makes a single obscene remark to you, or touches you in anyway..."

"He's been a military policeman and a security guard," she said dully. "I expect he knows the law backward and forward."

"Yes, ma'am, I'm sorry, because I imagine you're right. I wish we could do something."

"So do I. Thanks for listening."

She hung up and sat with her head down. She could call Lang, but she knew what he'd do. If Erikson could get Lang arrested, he'd have a clear field. She didn't want that. And he hadn't harmed her, yet. She had to keep her emotions under control. If she panicked and did something stupid, she'd be playing right into his hands.

But what could she do? She grabbed her purse and went back out to the parking lot. He was still there. She didn't look at him this time. She got into her car, locked the doors, started it and pulled out onto the street.

A glance in her rearview mirror told her that he was following her.

Well, she had a surprise in store for him this time. She'd spotted a police car cruising downtown. She deliberately pulled up beside it and watched as Erikson fell back. So he wasn't quite as confident as he made out. That was useful information.

When the police car turned, Kirry turned behind him. She followed him through the downtown area, with Erikson trailing behind. Then, without warning, she swung the wheel and turned down an alley, cut through and came in behind Erikson.

He was looking around for her, but he didn't seem to see her. Good. She had him where she wanted him.

He turned onto a secondary street and Kirry turned the other way. She'd lost him, just temporarily. It was a relief to know that she could do even that.

She went back to her building, parked the car in her spot, and rushed up to her apartment, quickly securing the door. *That's one for me, Erikson,* she thought.

A few minutes later, the telephone rang. She let the answering machine catch it, certain that it was an irate Erikson. But the voice on the other end was Lang's.

"Are you there, Kirry?" he asked.

She picked up the receiver and turned off the machine. "Yes, I am. Hi, Lang," she said.

"What the hell were you trying to do out there, incite him to violence?" he asked angrily. "You can't play games with a madman, Kirry!"

"You saw me!" she exclaimed.

"Of course I saw you," he muttered.

"But I didn't see you!"

"That's the first rule of shadowing someone—don't be seen."

She smiled. "I didn't know you were looking out for me. Thanks, Lang!"

"I won't always be there. I can't always," he said, "so please exercise some common sense and stop trying to outfox Erikson. He's no fool. He'll realize what you did, and it will make him angrier. Don't you understand that his sort can't bear being beaten by a woman? He takes it as a challenge to his manhood!"

"Well, poor him. What about me?" she stormed. "Do I have no rights at all? I hate having him follow me around and stare at me," she added furiously. "I called the police, and they said there wasn't a thing they could do. Not a thing! What if he kills me? Can they do something then?"

"You're getting too uptight, Kirry," he said. "Calm down. Use your mind. If he was going to hurt you, he'd have done it when I fired him. He's only trying to wear you down and freak you out, to make you hurt yourself or make a fool of yourself."

"That isn't what you said . . ."

"I didn't know," he replied. "Not at first. I'm still not certain enough to risk your life by guessing which way he'll jump. We'll handle it. I won't let him hurt you."

The calm confidence in his voice soothed her badly stretched nerves. "I know that."

"And when I'm through with you, you'll be able to take care of yourself. We'll have another lesson tomorrow night. Okay?"

She sighed. "Okay."

"Get some sleep. I'll be in touch."

He hung up and she smiled, thinking that maybe it would work out all right. She was just jumpy, that was all.

The phone rang, and she laughed as she picked it up.

"Forgot something, did you?" she teased.

"Yeah," a cold, too familiar voice replied. "I forgot to tell you that tricks like you played on me tonight won't work again."

"Leave me alone, Erikson!" she snapped. "You have no right . . . !"

"You got me fired, you snooty little tramp," he said. "No woman does that to me. I'm through playing games."

"Listen to me, you lunatic . . . !" she yelled back, but the line was already dead.

She put the receiver down with a slam, her face hot with temper. Damn him! What was she going to do?

Four

Kirry had never felt so threatened in her life. She left her apartment the next morning and found Erikson right in the front of the building, sitting in that blue sedan.

With a fury she couldn't contain, she picked up a rock from the landscaped cacti and flung it at the car with all her might. He ducked, shocked, but her pitching arm wasn't what it should have been. The rock fell short. By golly, she promised herself, the next one wouldn't. She picked up three big rocks and ran toward his car.

Before she could get started, he roared off, leaving her standing there, shaking. She fought for control of herself and slowly dropped the rocks, brushing off her hands. The man was crazy, she thought bitterly. Crazy! And she couldn't do a thing to stop him!

She got into her car and locked it and went to work. She knew the blue sedan would be sitting there, on the street, and sure enough, it was. She was shaking as she got out and locked her own car and started toward the building. There were no rocks in the landscaping here, nothing that she could throw at him. He smiled at her from cold eyes as she walked up the sidewalk toward her office building.

"You can't stop me from sitting here, and there aren't any rocks, baby," he called to her.

She stopped, her knees vibrating from fear and temper. She looked straight into his eyes. "If you don't stop now, you'll wish you had," she said quietly.

"Oh, yeah? What you gonna do, big bad girl?" he challenged.

"Wait and see, Mr. Erikson," she said, and smiled as if she had every confidence that he was going to wind up wearing prison blues.

She turned and walked into the building without looking back.

Mack's eyes narrowed as she passed him. "I saw him sitting there when I came in," he said. "I've phoned the new security chief and Mr. Lancaster. They're working on something."

"A bomb?" she asked pleasantly. "Because that's what it may take. He won't stop. The law can't touch him, and he knows it."

"Isn't your mother married to some rich person overseas?" Mack asked.

She didn't like talking about her mother. "She's married to a wealthy English nobleman."

"Well, couldn't he hire you a hit man?" he asked.

She burst out laughing. "Oh, for God's sake, will you stop watching those mob movies?" she mumbled, walking off into her own office.

"It's worth a thought!" he called after her.

She closed the door.

It was a busy day. She didn't go out for lunch, choosing instead to have one of the other women bring it to her. If Erikson wanted to sit out there and bake in his car all day, let him. She was going to try pretending that he was invisible. Perhaps Lang had been right—if Erikson meant to hurt her, he'd have done it by now. She just had to keep her nerve until he got tired of watching her and gave it up.

Lang was waiting for her when she got to her apartment. For once, Erikson hadn't followed her home. But she knew that he was out there somewhere, watching, always watching.

"Get your gi and let's go," Lang said as they reached her apartment. "I'm taking you out to dinner before we go to the gym."

"You don't have to..."

"Just a hamburger, Kirry, not a five-course meal," he said curtly. "There are some things we need to talk about."

"Okay." She got her things from the closet and turned on her answering machine.

He held her bag while she locked up the apartment. He seemed very preoccupied and not a little concerned. He hardly said a word all the way to a nearby hamburger joint, where they nibbled burgers and fries and drank coffee.

"You're worried, aren't you?" she asked.

He nodded. He sipped coffee, and his dark eyes narrowed over the cup as he studied her. "I had a friend of mine do some hard digging into Erikson's past. He was arrested for killing a man while he was an MP. He was acquitted, but people were generally sure that he did it. It was a racially motivated incident."

"Oh, boy," she said heavily.

"It gets worse," he added. "He's covered his tracks pretty good, or he'd never have gotten a job as a security officer. He's been in jail three different times on assault charges that were dropped because the witnesses refused to testify. The victims were women," he added quietly. "Young women. Two of them claimed that he raped them, but they were too afraid of him to go to court."

Kirry felt her face turning white. She wasn't a fearful person as a rule, but this was an extraordinary circumstance. She put down the rest of her half-eaten hamburger and fought to keep what she'd already eaten down.

"Your mother lives in Europe," he said. "I know you two don't get along, but it would benefit you to go over there and visit her for a few weeks until I can get something done about Erikson.''

"Run away, you mean?" she asked. "You're the second person today who's mentioned my mother, but Mack asked if her husband couldn't hire a hit man to deal with my problem."

He pursed his lips and his eyes twinkled. "What a magnificent suggestion."

"Stop that. You were a government agent."

"So I was, dash the luck." He leaned back in his chair and searched her face. "You won't go to Europe?"

She shook her head. "I'm not running. He's not going to make a coward out of me, no matter what he's done in the past."

He smiled. "You always did have guts, Kirry," he said, chuckling.

"Too many to suit you right now, huh?" she teased.

He caressed the paper cup that held a mouthful of warm coffee. "If you won't run, how about a compromise?"

"What did you have in mind?"

"Safety in numbers."

"I won't live at the YWCA," she said, outguessing him.

"That wasn't exactly what I had in mind."

She hesitated. She was doing it again; reading his mind. "You want me to move in with you. You're very sweet, Lang, but I couldn't...."

"I don't want to move in with you," he said bluntly. "I've explained the situation to your apartment manager, and he's giving me the apartment next door to you," he said calmly.

"Oh." She felt chastened. He made it very clear that living with her was not something he wanted to do. Maybe it wouldn't have been a good idea, but it hurt a little to think that he wouldn't even consider it.

"If you moved in with me, nobody would care," she said, surprising herself. "People don't sit in judgment over the moral values of their fellow man anymore."

"Want to bet?"

She felt and looked irritated. "All right, then, move in next door. I don't want you in my apartment, anyway. You'd seduce me," she accused, and was amazed that she could joke about it.

"You wish," he countered dryly. "I'm very particular about my body. You might have noticed that I keep it in rare good condition, and I'll tell you flat that it's in great demand by women. I don't share it with everyone who asks."

Her eyebrows lifted and her eyes twinkled. "You don't?"

His broad shoulders lifted and fell. "It's a dangerous practice these days, sleeping around," he reminded her with a quiet smile.

She smiled back. "Yes, I know. That's why I don't do it."

The smile was still there, but there was something somber in his dark eyes. "Ever come close?" he asked very softly.

She hesitated, and then shook her head. "Only with you, that one time," she said involuntarily, and her eyes flickered with painful memories before they fell.

He slid his hands deep into his pockets. He remembered, as she did, the wonder of that night. Nothing in his life before or since had ever equaled it, as relatively innocent an experience as it had been. Because he knew in his heart that he wasn't ready for marriage, he'd been too honorable to seduce a woman as innocent as Kirry, although their intimacy had been devastating just the same.

Then the very next day, Chad had dropped his bombshell and the relationship had shattered forever.

"You sit pretty heavy on my conscience sometimes," he said unexpectedly.

Her eyes lifted to his. "That's a shocker," she murmured. "I thought I was just one in a line."

"Fat chance." His gaze slid over her slowly, boldly. "I suggested that we get engaged, but I didn't really want to get married and you did. That was the real problem. I guess that's why I believed Chad, and not you."

"That's what my mother said."

"Well, she is astute every now and then," he observed.

"It was the only time in our lives that she really tried to act like my mother," she reminisced. "I needed her, and she was there. Even if it was a fairly innocent thing, it hurt once it was over.''

"Did you think I got away scot-free?" he asked curiously.

She shrugged. "You wanted out and you got out."

"I didn't want to get married," he repeated. "That didn't mean I wasn't involved emotionally. It hurt me, too.''

"That's hard to imagine," she said. "You never took anything seriously, least of all me.''

"You'd be surprised." He looked at her intently before continuing. "The apartment I'm getting isn't very large, but I like the view. And it's convenient to yours, if Erikson tries anything.''

She didn't like to think about that. Knowing what she'd learned about the man made her very nervous. "Couldn't we manage better if you moved in with me?" she said, thinking out loud. "I have two bedrooms and I can cook.''

"I can cook, too," he volunteered, ignoring her offer. "And I don't have a phobia of vacuum cleaners. This last one I bought has lasted a whole month.''

"A month!''

"Well, the damned things are like elephants. When you drag them around by the trunk and get them hung on furniture, and jerk real hard...it pulls their little trunks off!''

She laughed. He was as incorrigible as ever. He made her forget Erikson, even if just for a little while.

"Feel like helping me move tonight?''

"If we'll have enough time, I guess so." She had visions of lugging furniture up on the elevator as she toyed with her napkin. "Is there someone who'd mind if you stayed in my apartment?" she prompted, curious about his reasons for refusing.

"A woman, you mean?"

She nodded.

"No," he said gently. "There isn't anyone."

"I see."

"Probably not." He chuckled. "Finished? Let's go fall on a mat for a couple of hours."

"I'm still sore from the last time," she groaned.

"And we haven't even gotten to the bag, yet." He sighed. "You'll have to take more vitamins."

"It sure does look like it," she agreed grimly.

The side and back break falls went on forever, but this night he began to teach her the hand positions as well. The more she learned about economic movement, the more fascinating it became. She could understand how people loved the sport. There were several women in the gym this particular night, being taught a self-defense class by Tony, the man who managed the gym.

"They're doing a lot more than we are," she said pointedly to Lang while she was catching her breath.

"Sure they are. It's a two-week class. He has to get through a lot of material. And it's just basic stuff, like how to bring a high heel down on an instep or put a knee in a man's groin. You're learning a lot more, and it will take longer."

"Oh, I see."

"You're a promising pupil, too," he had to admit. "You're taking to it like a duck to water."

"Why didn't you ever show me any of this years ago, when we were together?" she asked.

He searched her curious eyes. "Because it was hard enough to keep my hands off you. A class like this, with constant touching, would have put me right over the edge."

Her eyebrows arched. "But you never wanted me." She blurted out the words. "Only that once...."

He moved closer, so that his voice wouldn't carry, so close that she could feel the strength and heat of his body. "I wanted you night and day," he said huskily. "You were too innocent to notice."

"I must have been," she agreed. "But it doesn't seem to bother you now."

"I'm older," he replied. "And a good deal more experienced."

Her eyes went cold. "Of course."

He turned away. The jealousy he saw in those green eyes made his body ache. She still felt possessive about him, but that didn't mean she still cared. He had to remember that, and not read too much into her reactions.

"Let's try this again."

He positioned her on the mat and invited her to use one of the hold-breaking positions on him. She went through the motions smoothly, but she couldn't get him onto the mat. He countered every move she made, laughing.

"That's not fair, Lang," she panted, pushing. "You won't cooperate."

"Okay, go ahead. Throw me." He relaxed, standing still.

She put her whole heart into it, stepping in with one leg, tripping with the other, pushing and pulling until she broke his balance and put him down. But she underestimated her own stability, and in the process, she went down heavily on top of him.

"You aren't supposed to fall *with* the victim," he instructed.

She was too winded to move momentarily. One of her legs was between both of his, her breasts flattened on his chest, her hands on either side of his head. It was a surprisingly comfortable position, if she'd been a little less aware of the intimacy of it.

"Could you help me up?" she asked breathlessly.

"Why not? You've certainly helped me up," he said with a blatant sensuality that brought a blush to her face when he shifted and made the point very clear.

"Lang!" she gasped.

He chuckled with pure delight as she scrambled off his body and got to her feet, red faced.

"Well, fortunately for us both, these jackets are loose and hip length," he said as he rose to tower over her.

"You're horrible!" she exclaimed, pushing back strands of damp blond hair from her eyes.

"You might consider it a form of flattery," he remarked. "Actually this condition isn't as easy to create as you might think. Not with other women, at least...."

"I want to go home," she said stiffly.

"Suit yourself, but you're going to miss the best part. I was going to teach you how to deal with a kick."

"You can do that another time," she said, fighting for composure.

"I was only teasing, Kirry," he said gently.

She let out a long sigh. "I'm not laughing," she muttered.

"Get your stuff and we'll drop by my apartment and get my stuff."

She hesitated. "Maybe he'll give it up."

He shook his head, and there was weary wisdom in his eyes. "Not a chance."

Lang's apartment was on the sixth floor of an old downtown hotel, and the decor was Roaring Twenties. It was dark and cramped, and Lang's belongings barely filled one suitcase.

"That's all?" she asked uneasily, lifting her eyes to his when he'd changed in the bedroom and came out with one suitcase and a long suit bag.

"That's it," he agreed. "I travel light."

"But you must have more than that!"

"I do. It's at Bob and Connie's place."

"Oh, of course. I forgot. You wouldn't want to carry heirlooms around the world with you."

"Speaking of heirlooms," he said slowly, "what did you ever do with the emerald I gave you?"

She averted her eyes. "Do you really think I'd keep something that reminded me of you, after the way you dumped me?"

"Yes, I do," he said.

She glared at him. "I meant to throw it away."

"I wouldn't have blamed you," he assured her. He smiled. "But I'm glad you didn't hate me enough to actually do it."

"It's a pretty ring," she commented.

"But you don't wear it."

"It's part of the past. I wanted to start over. I went to university and when I came out, with a major in public relations, I walked right into this job. I've been very lucky."

"You're alone," he remarked.

"I wanted it that way," she said shortly. "When I'm ready, I'll start looking for a husband."

"Have anyone in mind?" he asked carelessly, gathering his stuff.

"Mack," she said triumphantly.

He raised an eyebrow and grinned. "Do tell."

"Mack's settled and financially secure, and good company."

"You'd shrivel up like a prune if he touched you," he scoffed. "I've seen the way you draw your legs up when he comes close."

"You have not!"

"Kirry, you don't know a damned thing about modern surveillance techniques, do you?" he asked dryly. "Maybe that's good. I'd hate to make you inhibited when you dance around your bedroom in the nude."

She gasped audibly and went scarlet. "You Peeping Tom!"

"Accidental, I swear it," he said, holding up a hand. "It was the mirror. I had the camera just a little too far to the left...."

She aimed a blow at him, and he sidestepped just in time.

He laughed delightedly. "I thought you were spectacular," he said deeply. "All pink and mauve and blond. A nymph caught cavorting among the ferns. I didn't sleep all night long."

She glared at him. "I hate you."

"Kirry," he said softly, "I didn't see much that I haven't already seen before. I know, you don't like remembering that, but it's true."

"If I'd known what was going to happen later, that you'd believe those sick lies of Chad's...!"

"You'd never have let me touch you. I know that," he replied, his voice quiet and somber.

She wrapped her coat closer around her gi. "I'm ashamed of that night, anyway."

That stung. "I can't imagine why," he said matter-of-factly. "We were engaged. Most engaged people make love, and it isn't as if we went all the way."

"They make love when they actually plan to get married. That's why you always held back before, wasn't it, because you never had any intention of marrying me?"

"Once or twice, I thought about it," he confessed. "You were hungry for that damned ring, for the proposal. I humored you, because you wanted it that badly. But I knew that I'd be no good as husband material until I got the wanderlust out of me. I tried to tell you that, but you were so young."

"Young and stupid," she agreed. "And desperately in love."

He averted his eyes. "In love, hell," he said curtly. "You wanted to sleep with me."

"Of course I did, but it was much more than that," she argued.

"You were only eighteen," he returned, moving toward the door. "It's ancient history now, anyway, and we have more important things to think about."

"Sure." She opened the door for him, refusing to look up.

He went out, let her move past him and then turned off the lights and locked the door. Later, he'd have a talk with the manager about his brief absence, to make sure the man knew that he was only leaving temporarily. He'd pay the rent up in advance, too, just in case. With any luck, Erikson was going to be a bad memory in the near future.

Kirry held his clothes bag while he unlocked the apartment next to hers and opened the door. It was smaller than hers, but not much. It had a better view than hers did of the Alamo, and it looked as though it had just been decorated. It was done in greens and browns, and somehow it suited Lang.

"Yes, I like this," he remarked as he looked around. He glanced back at her. "We live close enough to share kitchen duty. You could cook one night and I could cook the next."

"That would be nice," she said.

"But you can't sleep over," he added sternly. "No use begging, it won't work. I don't allow women into the bedroom. It's too hard to get them out."

She smiled faintly. "I'll bet it is."

His eyebrow jerked. "Want to find out why?" he asked sensually.

"I have a pretty good idea," she replied, dropping her eyes. "You're a hard act to follow."

He turned back toward her with his hands deep in his pockets. "So are you," he replied honestly.

Her eyes scanned his broad face and she had to bite down hard to keep from begging him to kiss her. That way lay disaster, she reminded herself. She knew better than to encourage Lang.

She turned. "Well, I'll let you get settled. I'm tired and I want to go to bed."

He followed her to the door and opened it for her. "I've already checked out this place," he said. "The bedroom where you sleep is on the other side of the wall of mine. If you rap on the wall, I'll hear you. I don't sleep heavily, ever."

"Thanks. That's nice to know."

"Wear a gown, will you?" he asked on a groan. "I have to keep you under surveillance for your own protection. Don't make it any harder on me than you have to."

She glared at him. "I'll wear body armor, in fact," she said with a curt nod of her head. "Good night, Lang."

"Sleep well."

"I want a nice hot bath and..." She hesitated, her eyes shooting to his.

He sighed with resignation. "Okay, I'll cut the camera off when I hear water running, will that do?"

"You don't need a camera in the bathroom!" she exclaimed.

"That's odd, the last man we protected said the same thing," he told her frankly. "We got some very interesting pictures of him and his lady...."

"How is it that you're still alive?" she asked, exasperated.

"Not for lack of effort by irate taxpayers, that's for sure," he said with twinkling eyes. "Sleep well, little one. I'll be as close as a shout if you need me."

"You'll get a shout if you don't turn those cameras off," she informed him.

"Spoilsport," he muttered.

"I don't watch you take baths," she assured him.

He didn't smile as she expected him to. His dark eyes held hers until she felt her knees buckle. "Want to?" he asked softly.

Five

She glowered at him. "Fat chance," she said smartly.

He shrugged. "Your loss," he informed her with dancing eyes. "Keep the door locked."

She gave him a speaking look.

"Overkill, huh?" he teased as he went to the door and opened it. "How about riding in with me in the morning?" he suggested. "I can guarantee you won't see your blue sedan buddy while I'm around."

"He might take that as cowardice," she said simply.

"Listen," he replied, leaning back against the door, "you can push your body just so far before it gives out on you. Stress is dangerous. Don't let it get to the point that your nerves are shot. If you go in with me, it will take some of the pressure off. Don't you even realize how tense you are lately?''

She felt the coldness of her own hands with irritation. "Yes, I know, but I don't want to make him think I'm afraid, even if I am."

He smiled. "He won't. He'll assume that I've taken you over. It's the way that kind of man thinks."

"Well, I guess I could ride with you," she said. "As long as you don't really try to take me over."

His dark eyes narrowed and wandered over her as if they were caressing hands. "Could I, Kirry, if I worked at it?" he asked, and there was something unfamiliar in the glint of his eyes.

"Sorry, I'm immune," she replied pertly.

"To measles, maybe," he agreed. "But not to me. You still blush when I look at you, after all these years."

"Skin hysteria," she countered. "My pores are all allergic to you."

He chuckled. "Remember when we went to the park that time, and wound up with six lost little kids in tow? They wanted to know why you had freckles across your nose and I told them it was because you were allergic to ice cream."

"And they almost cried for me." She smiled back. "Oh, Lang, we had such good times." The expression in her eyes became sad. "You were my best friend."

He winced. "And you were mine. But several years ago, I was a bad marriage risk. You must have known it. There was so much I wanted to do with my life, things I couldn't have done with a family.''

"Yes. Like joining the CIA.'' She dropped her gaze to his broad chest, because she didn't want him to see the remnants of the terror in them. She hadn't known exactly where he was for years, except when Connie and Bob, with whom she was still friends, let slip little bits of information about his work. She'd worried and watched the whole time, afraid that he was going to be killed, that he'd come home in a box. The reality of seeing him again that first day he'd come to work for Lancaster, Inc., had knocked her legs out from under her. She was still reeling from the impact of knowing that he'd given up the old life. And wondering why he had.

"Kirry?'' he asked softly, interrupting her memories.

"What?''

He shook his head. "You weren't even listening, were you?'' he mused.

"I was thinking about how it was while you were away,'' she said involuntarily, scanning his eyes. "I read about covert operations in the newspapers and wondered if you were in the middle of them, if you were all right.'' She laughed. "Silly, wasn't it?''

His face hardened. "That was what I wanted to spare you.''

"You wanted to spare me the fear?'' Her green eyes wandered over his broad face. "And you thought you had. Of course, I stopped loving you the minute you walked away from me, right?''

He leaned back heavily against the wall. "Right," he said doggedly. "You hated me when I left."

She smiled sadly. "I thought I did," she agreed. "But it wasn't that easy to put you in the past, Lang. It took a long time. There were so many memories. Almost a lifetime of them." She turned away. "I guess it's different for men. It's only physical with you."

"Why do you say that?"

"It's true. Men think with their glands, women with their hearts."

"That's stereotyping," he accused. "Men feel things as deeply as women do."

"You wanted me, but you couldn't bring yourself to do anything about it," she said. "If you'd loved me enough, you couldn't have walked away."

"You let me walk away," he said shortly. "You could have opened that damned letter I sent you!"

"Did it say something besides goodbye?" she asked, her voice harsh. "I thought it was another accusation, that you figured you hadn't said enough about my lack of character and morals."

He stuck his hands into his pockets. "I knew about Chad by then. I'd had time to get my priorities straight."

"I didn't know that," she reminded him. "All I knew was that when you left, you held me in contempt and never wanted to see me again. You said so—explicitly."

His eyes narrowed with painful memory. "I'd never had to handle jealousy before," he said. "It was new to me. Besides that, I felt betrayed. Chad was my best friend."

"Oh, why rehash it?" she muttered, turning away. "You wanted a way out and he gave you one, that's it in a nutshell. I hope you enjoyed your stint with the government, Lang. What I can't understand is why you gave it up and came back."

His dark eyes slid over her hungrily. "Can't you?"

She ignored the caress in his voice. "I'm tired," she said over her shoulder. "I'll see you in the morning."

"That you will." He opened the door. "And you're riding in with me, whether you want to or not." He closed the door on her openmouthed expression.

She picked up a vase and almost—almost—flung it at the closed door. But it would only mean a cleanup that she was too tired to do. Arguing with Lang wasn't going to change anything, and she didn't have enough nerve left to dwell on a dead past.

She started past her answering machine and noticed that it was blinking. She didn't want to listen to the messages, because one of them was probably Erikson. But her job sometimes infringed on her free time, because clients often called at night when they had more time to talk. She couldn't afford to ignore the calls.

Grimacing, she pushed the Replay button.

The first message was from Mack, reminding her that he was bringing in a new client for her to work with the next morning and to be on time. The second was a wrong number.

The third, as she'd feared, was Erikson. "One night, your bodyguard won't be close by, and I'll get you." He purred. "What are you going to do then, Your Highness?"

The line went dead. She took out the tape and replaced it with another one. That nasty little remark might come in handy in court if Erikson made a wrong step. She slipped it into a drawer and went to bed, to toss and turn all night.

When Lang rang her doorbell the next morning, she was dressed in a neat lavender dress with a patterned scarf. He was wearing a gray sport coat with tan slacks and a red-and-white striped shirt. He looked very nice, but she pretended not to notice.

"Here," she said, handing him the tape from her answering machine. She told him what it was.

He slipped it into his pocket with cold eyes. "He'll overstep one day soon," he promised her. "And when he does, I'll be right there waiting."

"He's sick, isn't he?" she asked.

"Sick, or just plain damned mean," he replied. He waited while she locked her door and escorted her out to his car in the parking lot.

"Wait a minute," he said, holding her back before she could open the door.

He went around and did a quick check of the car, even under the hood. Satisfied, he opened the door and helped her inside.

"What was that all about? You don't think he'd go so far as to blow up your car?" she asked.

He shrugged as he pulled out into traffic. "Caution is worth its weight in gold sometimes, and you never know which way a man like that is going to jump."

"I see."

He glanced at her with a smile. "Don't look so worried. I can defuse a bomb."

"Can you really?"

He nodded. "If it's a simple one. There was this case in Europe, when we were..." He hesitated. "Well, that's classified. But I had to defuse a bomb, just the same."

"Is that something they taught you?" she asked, curious.

He chuckled. "No. It's something I learned the hard way."

Her eyes were saucer-big. "The hard way?"

"Sure, by getting blown up." He glanced at her expression amusedly. "Kirry, it was a joke. I'm kidding!"

She made a futile gesture with her hands. "I never could tell when you were," she said, shaking her head. "I guess I'm hopelessly naive," she muttered, glaring down at the purse in her lap. "At least I can fall down pretty good, though," she added brightly.

"Sure you can. And when I get you through the basics of self-defense, you'll be a holy terror on the street. Grown men will run from you screaming," he promised. "I can't imagine why you haven't done that before. Every woman should know how to take care of herself. They should teach it in school."

"They have enough to do in school without that."

"No kidding, it could be part of gym class in high school, physical education. Mothers could stop worrying so much about their girls if they knew how to foil an attacker." He glanced at her. "That includes an overamorous date."

"I have heard of date rape, thanks," she returned.

He chuckled. "In our case, I was the one with all the worries. You were one eager woman."

"Go ahead, rub it in," she grumbled, shifting away from him.

"How can I help it? You were beautiful, and you wanted me. You could have had anybody."

"Not quite, or you'd never have gotten away," she said, tongue in cheek. It was getting easier to handle the old rejection, now that she and Lang were friends again.

"Think so?" He parked the car just outside her office building, glancing around. "No Erikson," he said, nodding. "Good. Maybe he's terrified and gave it up."

"Right," she said dryly.

"I could get testimonials from people I've protected who'll tell you I'm terrifying," he informed her haughtily. "This last guy, in fact, said that it was a miracle we still had a country with people like me guarding it."

She laughed. "The man whose bathroom you bugged?" she asked.

"They said to watch him all the time," he replied. "So I watched him. *All* the time."

She just shook her head. Then she remembered that he was watching *her* all the time, too. Her eyes spoke for her.

"Not in the bathroom," he said. "Not when the door is opened or closed. Scout's honor."

"You were never a scout," she countered.

"I was until I started my first fire." He sighed, remembering. "Unfortunately it was in the scoutmaster's living room, on his carpet. Never could get him to understand how that accident happened. It was Bob's fault, anyway," he added darkly. "Bob was the one who gave me the stuff to do it with and showed me how."

"Did Bob like the scoutmaster?"

"Come to think of it, he didn't."

She chuckled. "I see."

They got out of the car and Lang's hand slid into hers as they walked toward the building. He felt her jerk and his fingers contracted. He stopped and looked down at her.

"Too good to hold hands with the hired help, are we?" he murmured dryly.

She felt his big fingers caressing hers and his thumb found its way to her soft palm. It was starting all over again, the magic she'd felt when he came close.

"No," she answered softly, looking straight up into his eyes. "But I don't want to relive the past."

"Not even with a different ending?" he asked softly. "A happy ending this time?"

Her heart skipped. It was just a game, she told herself. Lang was playing and she was letting herself take him seriously.

She began to laugh and tugged at her hand. "Let me go, you tease," she murmured.

He looked stunned. "Kirry, it's not . . ."

The sudden roar of a car engine caught his attention. He jerked Kirry onto the curb just as an old, dark-colored sports car swept by on the road.

"Lunatic," Lang said angrily, glaring after the car. If it had been a blue sedan, he'd have gone right after it.

"Careless drivers are everywhere," she said, brushing down her skirt. "I'm all right. He missed me by a mile."

"Not quite." He was pale. His eyes went over her like hands. "That was too close."

"At least it wasn't our friend Erikson," she said.

Lang nodded, but he wasn't convinced. He took her arm and escorted her into the building.

Later, he took out his laptop and plugged in with a secret access code. He called up Erikson's name and did some cross-checking. He closed the terminal a few minutes later feeling angry and sick. Erikson had two vehicles. One was an old black sports car.

Kirry had a long day. Part of it was taken up with a staff meeting and the rest would have dragged on endlessly, because she was caught up with all her current projects. Mack had promised her a new client first thing this morning, but the client had a conflict in her schedule, so they'd postponed it until the next day.

Betty stopped by her office that afternoon. "How's the new client?" she asked with a grin.

"I don't know. She didn't show. Mack said we'd try again tomorrow morning," she replied.

"I was going to suggest that we go out to a movie, but I guess that's not a good idea, with Mr. Nasty on the prowl."

"Lang would have a screaming fit," she agreed.

"He's good-looking," Betty ventured. "And there's no competition there."

"None that I can see," Kirry replied. "In the old days, it was a different story. When Lang and I started going together, he'd just broken up with his current heartthrob. She was a dish, too, a model. Lorna McLane."

Betty frowned. "Lorna McLane?"

Kirry stared at her. "What do you know that I don't know, Betty?"

"The name of the client who didn't show up this morning. It's Lorna McLane."

Kirry sat down. "What does she want with us?"

"She's worked her way up the ladder to an executive position at a local model agency that specializes in south Texas location work. Mack says that she wants us to coordinate a fashion show for her, publicity and all."

"Well, we can't afford to turn down something of that magnitude," Kirry said. "Besides, she and Lang were all washed-up before he and I even started dating. Not that it would matter anymore," she added quickly when she noticed Betty watching her. "Lang and I are just friends now. He's our security chief. That's all."

Betty studied her ringless left hand. "Lorna and Mrs. Lancaster are good friends, did you know?"

Kirry's heart stopped. "Good enough that Mrs. Lancaster might have told her about Lang's new job?"

The other woman nodded. "In fact, good enough friends that she told Lang about the job and put in a good word for him with her friend, Mrs. Lancaster."

So that was how he'd managed to get the job. "Nobody ever tells me anything," Kirry muttered darkly, hating the world and fate for playing such a monumental joke on her.

"I'm sure everybody meant to. Listen, just because Lang works here, it doesn't mean that Lorna will be hanging on his sleeve all the time. You can lead a horse to water..."

"Spare me." Kirry sighed and leaned back in her chair. She'd entertained false hopes and now they were being dashed. She felt depressed. Erikson was going to

destroy her peace of mind, and here was Lorna to aid
and abet him. She remembered the woman all too well;
she was tall and slender with very dark eyes and hair.
She was beautiful. If she still looked as she had when
Lang left her, it wasn't beyond the realm of reason that
Lang might be tempted to try his luck again. After all,
there was nothing to stop him. Lorna was presumably
unmarried, and so was Lang. And Kirry...well, she
was right off the menu. She wasn't bad looking, but she
couldn't compete with a top model. And while Kirry
was old-fashioned, Lorna had never been saddled with
cautious habits.

"You can't quit," Betty told her, reading her expression. "For one thing, I'd have nobody to go out to
lunch with."

"I won't promise not to," she said stubbornly. She
glared out the window. "Did you ever have one of
those spells where everything seemed to go wrong in the
space of a week?" she asked.

Betty let out a long breath. "I'm going to get you a
cup of coffee," she said, turning around. "It isn't on
my job description, but I think I know my way around
a coffeepot."

"Betty, why did Lorna pick this agency when there
are several in San Antonio? Was it because of Lang, do
you think?"

"If I were a betting woman, that would be first on
my list," the other woman had to admit. "Still carrying a torch for Lang?"

Kirry glared at her. "I am not. I don't even like Lang."

"And pigs fly," Betty said under her breath as she went out and closed the door behind her.

Lang picked Kirry up late that afternoon, his eyes cautious and wary as he looked around the parking lot.

"I haven't seen a blue sedan all day," Kirry told him as they drove out of the parking lot.

"Or an old black sports car?" he asked.

She frowned. "There *was* a black car." His expression gave him away. He looked resigned. "Don't tell me," she said sardonically. "Erickson has two cars, and one of them is black."

"Bingo."

"This just hasn't been my day."

"Why?"

She looked at him and felt her life going into eclipse. It would be the old story, all over again, Lang walking away from her.

"Did you know that we're getting a new client at the agency?" she asked instead.

"If that expression is anything to go by, it must be someone I know. Do we play twenty questions, or do you just want to spit it out?"

"Lorna McLane is going to let us promote her new modeling extravaganza."

He didn't look at her. She knew. He was sure of it. "Well, good for her."

Kirry didn't move a muscle. She went right on staring through the windshield as if she'd taken root in the seat. "You knew she was here."

He shrugged. "Yes, I knew. How do you think I got this job?" he asked. "She phoned me in D.C., said that it was on offer and suggested that I apply. You might remember that Lorna and I were an item before you and I started going together," he reminded her gently. "But it was never that serious. Then," he added to madden her.

She felt her heart drop. "Have you seen her since you've been back?" she asked, trying to sound casual.

He speared a glance toward her, finding her brooding expression enlightening. "We had lunch today, in fact," he admitted, smiling at the venomous look in Kirry's face at the remark. "She's a little older, but still a knockout. Pretty as a picture, in fact."

Kirry clutched her bag and stared out the side window.

He felt ten feet tall. There was hope. She did still care! "Don't forget. We're having another lesson tonight."

"But I thought we were doing that tomorrow night," she asked abruptly.

"It was. Erikson's making me nervous," he said. "I think a good workout might benefit us both. How about you?"

She couldn't disagree. It would take her mind off at least one of her problems.

"You and Lorna almost got married once, didn't you?" she asked.

"She wanted to be a model and I wanted to be a government agent," he said easily, pulling up to the apartment building they shared. "She made some demands and I made some, then we both decided that a parting of the ways was the best idea." He turned off the engine and looked at her, his dark eyes somber. "I wanted a career more than I wanted anything at that time. I'm not really sorry, in a way. I've done a lot of exciting things, Kirry. I've grown up."

"It shows," she replied. There were lines in his face that had never been there in the old days. He had a new maturity, along with the clowning personality. "But I liked you just the way you were."

"I liked you," he returned, smiling. "You used to be a lot more spirited and full of fun. You've gone quiet on me, Kirry."

"I have a lot of responsibility with this new job," she said evasively. "And Erikson's been on my mind." She didn't add that it was killing her to be around Lang all the time, with the anguish of the past between them.

"He's been on my mind as well. But he'll make a slip, I promise you, and when he does, I'll be standing right next to him."

"Or I will," she said darkly. "Are we ever going to get to do anything besides fall on a mat?" she added plaintively. "I want to learn how to do something!"

"What did you have in mind?" he asked in a deliberately seductive voice, and leaned toward her with mock menace.

"Learning how to break somebody's arm would do nicely," she said, smiling.

He shivered. "As long as it isn't mine!"

"Would I damage my friend?" she chided. "Shame on you!"

They went to the gym, and Lang was aware, as Kirry wasn't, that they were being followed again. He wanted nothing more than to stop the car and get out, and beat the devil out of Erikson. But that would be playing right into the man's hands. He had to play a cool and careful hand here, or he could put Kirry in even more danger.

Meanwhile, it was going to be a very good idea to teach her some damaging moves.

They did the warm-up exercises, and went through the hand positions. Then Lang began to teach her escape maneuvers.

"This is boring," she muttered when he had her break a choke-hold for the tenth time.

"Pay attention," he replied tersely. "This isn't a game. Pretend that it's for real, and act accordingly."

She tried to, but her hands were getting tired.

"Okay, honey, if this is the only way I can get through to you..."

His hands tightened, and he moved in with a menacing expression. Kirry panicked, but she kept her

GOOD NEWS! You can get up to FIVE GIFTS—FREE!

If offer card is missing, write to:
Silhouette Reader Service, 3010 Walden Ave., P.O. Box 1867, Buffalo, NY 14269-1867.

▶ DETACH AND MAIL CARD TODAY!

NO POSTAGE
NECESSARY
IF MAILED
IN THE
UNITED STATES

BUSINESS REPLY MAIL
FIRST CLASS MAIL   PERMIT NO 717   BUFFALO, NY

POSTAGE WILL BE PAID BY ADDRESSEE

SILHOUETTE READER SERVICE
3010 WALDEN AVE
PO BOX 1867
BUFFALO NY 14240-9952

LUCKY CARNIVAL WHEEL

▼ SCRATCH-OFF GAME! ▼

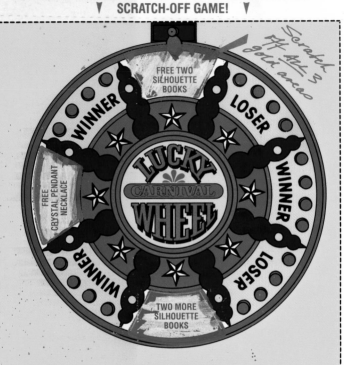

Scratch
off all 3
gold areas

FREE TWO SILHOUETTE BOOKS

WINNER

LOSER

FREE CRYSTAL PENDANT NECKLACE

LUCKY CARNIVAL WHEEL

WINNER

WINNER

LOSER

TWO MORE SILHOUETTE BOOKS

▼ DETACH AND MAIL CARD TODAY! ▼

YES! I have scratched off the 3 Gold Areas above. Please send me all the gifts for which I qualify. I understand I am under no obligation to purchase any books, as explained on the opposite page.

225 CIS ANDM
(U-SIL-D-01/94)

NAME

ADDRESS   APT.

CITY   STATE   ZIP

HOW TO PLAY:

1. With a coin, carefully scratch off the 3 gold areas on your Lucky Carnival Wheel. You could get one or more free Silhouette Desire® novels and possibly another gift, depending on what is revealed beneath the scratch-off areas.

2. Return your Lucky Carnival Wheel game card, and we'll immediately send you the books and gift you qualify for ABSOLUTELY FREE!

3. Then, unless you tell us otherwise, every month we'll send you 6 additional novels to read and enjoy, months before they're available in stores. You can return them and owe nothing. But if you decide to keep them, you'll pay only $2.49* each — plus 25¢ delivery and applicable sales tax, if any.* That's the complete price, and compared to cover prices of $2.99 each in stores — quite a bargain!

4. Your satisfaction is always guaranteed and you may cancel at any time just by dropping us a note or by returning any shipment at our cost. Of course, the FREE books and gift remain yours to keep!

No Cost! No Risk!
No Obligation to Buy!

PLAY THE

LUCKY
CARNIVAL
WHEEL

GAME...

GET AS MANY AS FIVE GIFTS FREE!

PLAY FOR FREE! NO PURCHASE NECESSARY!

nerve. Using the technique he'd taught her, she broke his handhold around her neck, stepped in, broke his balance and pushed him neatly onto the mat.

He rolled as gracefully as a ball, got to his feet in a combat stance and rushed her, his hand raising sharply in a side hand position. He gave a harsh, sharp yell and brought his hand down.

Kirry did what came naturally. She threw her hands over her face and screamed.

There were chuckles from the other side of the gym, from men who'd seen Lang use that shock tactic on young cops he was training, years ago.

Kirry caught her breath and swatted angrily at Lang. "You animal!" she raged. "That wasn't fair!"

"People are born with two natural fears," he informed her. "Fear of sudden, sharp noises and fear of falling. A sharp cry can temporarily paralyze, as you saw. That's one of the methods I like to teach. Sometimes just the yell is enough to buy you some time."

"It's very unpleasant to be on the receiving end of it!"

"I don't doubt it. But getting used to the idea of an attack might save you one day."

She saw his point. She was still getting her breath, and her heartbeat was frantic.

"Had enough?" he taunted, bringing back her fighting spirit.

"Not on your life," she told him shortly. "If you can take it, I can take it. Do your worst!"

He proceeded to, grinning all the way.

Six

——————

Kirry slumped beside Lang on the mat after an hour of exercises in breaking handholds, balance and repelling attacks. She could barely breathe at all, and every bone in her body felt as if it had taken a beating.

"Giving up?" he teased.

"Only for the moment," she said, panting. Her face was red and her hair was all awry. Lang thought she looked like a charming urchin.

"Remember the day we went swimming in the river?" he reminded with a gentle smile. "You almost drowned because you wouldn't admit that you couldn't last long enough to get across. I had to tow you back."

"I almost made it," she said, recalling the incident.

"And on the way back," he said, lowering his voice as he bent to stare into her eyes, "your top came off."

She felt the impact of his gaze as she'd felt it that day, when she'd experienced her first intimacy. Lang's eyes on her bare breasts had made her blush all over, had made her heart run like a mad thing. He hadn't embarrassed her, or made fun of her plight. He'd lifted her very slowly out of the water and looked at her; just that, then he'd put her back down, found her top and turned his back while she put it on again. It had been so natural and tender that she'd never regretted the experience.

"I remember the look on your face most of all," he continued quietly. "You were shocked and delighted and excited, all at the same time. An artist would have gone nuts trying to capture your expressions."

"It was the first time," she replied simply. "I was all those things. Of course, it wasn't unique for you."

"Wasn't it, Kirry?" He wasn't smiling, and his eyes were dark with secrets.

She averted her face. "Well, it was a long time ago. We're different people now."

He thought of all the places he'd been, all the adventures he'd had. He thought about the close calls and Kirry's laughing eyes, suddenly filled with tears because he wouldn't believe her the one time when it really mattered.

"I failed you," he said aloud.

"You wouldn't have been happy tied to me," she said, looking back at him. "You wanted your freedom too badly. That's why it didn't work out for you with me or Lorna."

His eyes narrowed. "Lorna was different," he said shortly. "She knew from the beginning that I wasn't interested in marriage, and she took me on those terms. But I never laid any conditions on the line with you. I didn't even really rule out marriage at first."

"Until you thought I'd slept with Chad." She finished the thought for him. "And that hurt your pride more than your heart."

"Love comes hard to some men, Kirry." He searched her eyes for a long moment. "And settling down..." His voice trailed off as he remembered, without wanting to, his own childhood.

"I knew you weren't ready." She dredged up a smile. "And despite the fact that you'd proposed, I wouldn't have married you, knowing that you really wanted the Company more than me. It was nice to pretend, though."

"Kirry," he began slowly, "I asked you once how you'd feel about trying again. You never really answered me. I wasn't kidding."

Her heart leaped, but her expression was wary. "I don't know, Lang."

"We could start from where we left off," he told her. "You're a woman now, not a girl just past adolescence. We can have a full relationship, without any of the hang-ups."

"You mean, we could sleep together, don't you?" she asked bluntly.

He stretched out his leg and studied it, not looking at her. "Yes. That's what I mean."

"I thought so." She reached into her bag for her shoes and socks and began putting them on, without answering.

"Well?" he asked shortly.

Her eyebrows lifted. "Well, what?"

"How would you feel about starting over?"

"I don't like glueing broken mirrors back together," she told him. "And you know how I feel about sleeping around already."

"It wouldn't be sleeping around," he said angrily. "You'd only be sleeping with me."

"For how long, Lang?" she asked matter-of-factly, her green eyes boring into his. "Until you had your fill?"

He saw the bitterness in her eyes. "You're twisting my words."

"No, I'm not. You need a woman, and I'm handy," she said, her eyes glittery with anger. "Thanks. Thanks a heck of a lot, Lang, it's so flattering to have a man look at me and see a half-hour's entertainment!"

She got to her feet and so did he, feeling frustrated and angry. She wouldn't let him finish. It seemed as if she didn't want him to make any serious propositions. On the other hand, she didn't want or love him enough to settle for just him, without the promise of permanent ties. That had always been the barrier between them, and it was still firmly in place. Kirry didn't trust him.

"Let me tell you something," she continued hotly, "when I want a man to sleep with, I'll find my own. And it won't be some hotshot with a string of ex-lovers! I wouldn't sleep with you if you had a medical certificate signed by the surgeon general!"

She picked up her bag and walked past him toward the entrance.

"Hold it right there," he said when he caught up with her and blocked her way. His face was livid, but he was in perfect control of his temper. "You go nowhere without me at night, or have you forgotten your 'other' beau?"

She hesitated. Anger suddenly became less important than the fact that Erikson could be out there waiting for her.

"I'm glad you've used your sense," Lang replied curtly. "Wait until I've changed and I'll take you home. After that, except for doing my job, you and I are quits. Happy?"

"Ecstatic," she said with a forced careless smile. "I don't have to have a man in my life. I get along very well on my own."

"So do I," he responded. "But if I get desperate, there's always Lorna. And she was never the old-fashioned type."

With that parting stroke, which went right through her heart, he sauntered off to get changed. Just as she thought, he was going back to Lorna. Well, he needn't think that she was going to stand around bleeding to death emotionally because he couldn't make a commitment.

She stared down at the gi bag with dead eyes. She'd hoped that Lang might be different, but those years abroad hadn't changed his basic attitudes at all. He still didn't need anyone in his life permanently, while Kirry couldn't survive a loose relationship. She was too intense, too possessive to live with the constant knowledge that she was just a pastime. Lang would take her for granted, use her and cast her off like a worn-out shoe. And where would she be then? With her heart broken all over again, that's where.

Lang was back five minutes later. He looked fresh and cool despite the frantic activity of the past hour. Kirry, by comparison, felt sticky and sweaty. She followed him out to the car in silence and climbed in on the passenger side.

With quiet caution, Lang checked the car out before he got in and started it. Even in his present mood, he couldn't let himself forget how unbalanced Erikson was. A man like that was a cunning enemy. It wouldn't do to become lax.

He left Kirry at her door with a good-night that was just barely civil—like hers to him—and went to bed uncommonly early. He hadn't wanted to start a fight with her over the past or the present. He wanted to settle down; it was why he'd come back here in the first place.

But Kirry wouldn't listen. Perhaps she didn't want to. Her career might be all she needed now, and just because she was jealous of Lorna, that didn't ensure that she was in love with him.

He'd exaggerated his relationship with Lorna, just to irritate Kirry. Lorna had been a delightful fling years ago, and she'd no more been serious than Lang had. She was still a pretty woman, and he found her attractive. But Kirry had his heart. The thing was, she didn't want it anymore. Even less did she want him. That was what had angered him so much, when just looking at her made him go rigid with desire.

Well, he wasn't going to worry himself into a fit about it. He'd cross the bridges when he came to them. He rolled over and closed his eyes. What he needed now was sleep. Plenty of sleep.

For days on end, there was no sign of Erikson at all. It was a shock to Kirry, who looked for him everywhere with nervous apprehension. But as time went by, and there were no more phone calls or surveillance from him, she slowly became complacent. She was happy, too, because she believed that he'd given up. Maybe he'd put it all into perspective and decided that harassing her wasn't worth the possible cost to himself. It even made sense—if he wasn't playing some psychological game with her, that was, lulling her into a false sense of security. She grew cautiously optimistic, though, when nothing happened.

Erikson's absence was the only thing that gave her cause for pleasure, however, because she'd landed Lorna's account. That meant she had to spend considerable amounts of time with Lorna, who was now dating Lang again. And Lorna apparently felt obliged to share every little detail with Kirry.

"I do like the idea of making this ribbon-cutting appearance, dear," Lorna purred as they conferred over a business lunch. "But it mustn't interfere with my private life. They'll simply have to change it to the afternoon. Lang is taking me to the opera."

Kirry didn't betray her feelings by even the batting of an eyelash, but she was certain that the durable plastic smile she reserved for Lorna was going to be on her lips when she was buried.

"I'll see what I can do," she promised the other woman, mentally anticipating being cussed out royally by the business in question. She would have to do some really fast talking to get them to agree to what Lorna wanted. Even then, they might not cooperate.

"Good. And one more thing, Kirry, is it absolutely necessary for you to have an apartment next door to Lang's?" she asked with visible irritation. "It seems to inhibit him when we're together."

"He moved next door to me because of the threats an ex-employee here was making," she told Lorna. She didn't mention that Lang made sure she heard him bringing Lorna to his apartment every other night. Or that hearing the two of them laughing next door, after midnight, had left her sleepless for the past four days. "Since the threat no longer seems to exist, I don't see why Lang couldn't move back to his old place." In fact, she'd be delighted if he left. Then she would at

least be spared the audible evidence of Lang's pleasure in Lorna's company.

"I knew you'd agree! I told him it wouldn't hurt
your feelings if I made the suggestion to you! Men are
such cowards about women's emotions, aren't they?"

So she'd been discussing it with Lang, had she? Kirry
was as angry as she was hurt. "He might have asked me
himself," she said.

"Oh, he couldn't bring himself to do that." Lorna
dismissed it. "But when I tell him, he'll be pleased."

"I'm sure he will."

"Now, about the network coverage, do you think
you could get CNN to come...?"

By the end of the day, Kirry was totally washed-out.
She couldn't remember ever feeling quite so bad.

Lang had stopped by just briefly, a stranger with his
cold face and eyes. He hardly spoke to her at all lately
unless he had to. He was remote and polite. She knew
that he was still keeping her under surveillance for her
safety's sake, but there was nothing personal about it,
and no warmth in him. Kirry grieved all over again for
the past. Why couldn't he have stayed out of her life?
she wondered miserably.

He'd stuck his head into her office door just to tell
her that she'd be on her own that one afternoon, as he
was to meet Lorna at a local restaurant for a quick
dinner. He cautioned her about watching out for Erikson, which led to a heated exchange of words. It was a
relief when he left. She could function, she told her-

self, without someone shadowing her. She really felt that way. Until she got to her car.

Erikson was sitting in the front seat. She came to a sudden halt and gaped at him. He was back. She wasn't safe. He hadn't given up. She could have cried. It was going to start all over again, and she felt her stomach tying itself in knots as she wondered how she was going to cope with this.

"Hello, sweet thing," he said with a cold smile. "Did you think I'd forgotten you?"

"Get out of my car!"

"Make me," he challenged.

She knew better than to try that. Erikson was a trained security officer. Her few hold-breaking routines might work on a novice, but he probably had a colored belt, and hers was still white. Knowing when to back off was as important, Lang had once told her, as knowing when to attack. And you never attacked; you waited for the opponent to come at you, which gave you the advantage. All these thoughts worked through her mind while she stared at the man occupying her car. "Okay, Mr. Erikson. I'll let the police extricate you for me."

She turned and went quickly back toward the building, red faced with temper. As she got to the door, she heard a car door slam. She whirled. Erikson had left her car and was on the way to his. As she watched, he got into it and drove slowly away, tooting the horn as he reached the corner.

For a moment she wavered, wondering if she should call the police anyway. But it would hardly do any good, when he was no longer there.

She walked back to her car and opened the door, just in time to see the grenade on the floorboard. She gasped and started to step back, but it exploded. She covered her eyes instinctively, expecting the concussion to knock her backward, but it was only a gas grenade. There was a loud noise that hurt her ears, then her car filled with noxious fumes and she got out of the way in time to escape everything except a stinging pain in her eyes and throat. The fumes made her cough.

It was the last straw. Damn Erikson! Sobbing with bad temper, she got into the building and called 911. Minutes later, two police officers arrived. Lang was just behind them.

He started toward her, grim-faced, but she resisted the need for comfort. She turned to the first police officer who reached her and told him exactly what had happened.

Lang stood by, his face hard and unreadable, and listened while she talked and then answered questions.

"He's long gone, now," she said miserably. "I didn't think he'd try to hurt me...."

"If he'd wanted to do that, it would have been a hand grenade, not a gas grenade," the young patrolman assured her. "But this qualifies under the terroristic threats and acts law, and we can also get him for breaking and entering."

"If we can get any prints off the car," an older officer amended quietly. He looked at Kirry. "Was he wearing gloves?"

She remembered Erikson's hands on the wheel, and as they flashed into her consciousness, she remembered the black covering on them.

"Yes," she said miserably.

"There goes the case. It's your word against his," the older man said.

"But . . . !"

"It's the way the law's written," he said irritably. "None of us like it. Do you have any idea how many creeps prey on women and get away with it because we can't do anything to help them? God, I'd give anything for a stalking law with teeth, but we haven't got one yet! You aren't the only victim, although I expect it feels that way right now."

"It does."

"Watch this guy," the older police officer said suddenly. "You shouldn't have been out here alone."

Lang's face went hard and he actually flinched. "No, she shouldn't have," he agreed. "I'm chief of security here, and I thought he'd given it up. My mistake."

"It could have been a fatal one, for her," the older man said brutally.

Lang's eyes were anguished. "Don't you think I know that?" He gritted out the words.

Something in his expression made the other man leave it alone. He apologized once again to Kirry and left with his partner.

"I have to drive it home," Kirry said dully.

"You do not. We'll lock it and leave it. For one thing, it will have to be cleaned before you can drive it again."

"Oh. Yes, I see, I hadn't realized . . ." She went to lock it, feeling numb from the brain down.

Lang helped her into his car and drove her back to her apartment. "I'm sorry," he said through his teeth.

"It isn't your job to watch just me all the time," she said patiently. "You have lots of people to protect."

"I really thought he was through. It's been almost two weeks since we've even seen him. I acted like a green agent, not like a professional. I heard the call over the city band on my scanner on the way back to the office. I had no idea what I'd find when I got here. I should have known!" His hand hit the steering wheel hard with impotent rage.

His pride was hurt, she decided. He'd fallen down on the job because his mind had been on Lorna. He didn't have to say so, but Kirry knew it. She stared out the window until he parked the car, and then she followed him inside the building and up on the elevator without a word.

She turned to him outside her apartment, feeling haggard and worn-out. "Thanks for bringing me home."

He scowled. "Are you going to be all right?"

"Of course. I'm not bric-a-brac," she chided. "I won't break."

"Keep your doors locked," he said. "And don't stand near any windows."

"You're getting paranoid," she muttered. "He isn't going to come at me with a high-powered rifle."

"I don't know what he's going to do," he said grimly, running a hand through his thick hair. "But we're not going to get careless again. Got that?"

"I wasn't careless. I looked, and I didn't see anybody anywhere in the parking lot," she said angrily. "I didn't see him until I was standing right next to the car. I didn't go close enough to get grabbed."

"What if he'd had a gun, Kirry?" he asked in a haunted tone.

"Oh, for God's sake, he isn't going to shoot me!"

He didn't answer her, or smile. He was seeing her lying facedown on the pavement, her eyes open, her body broken from gunfire. He'd seen other agents go that way. He knew, as Kirry didn't, how unpredictable people like Erikson were.

"I'm all right," she said, driven to reassure him. "Don't go off the deep end, Lang, I'm fine." She hesitated. "And if you want to move out, I've already told Lorna it's all right with me. I'm not afraid...."

He frowned. "What the hell are you talking about?"

"Lorna told me that you were getting tired of having to live next door to me," she said. "She must be insecure, because I get every little detail of what you do with her."

"I didn't say anything to her about moving out of here," he told her angrily. "I wouldn't even consider it until this Erikson situation is resolved, one way or the other.''

That made her feel light-headed with joy. Lorna had lied. He didn't want to get rid of her!

"I didn't know that she was having that much contact with you," he said curtly.

"I'm having to handle her account," Kirry told him. "The others jumped out windows and hid in rest rooms until I got saddled with her. She's a perfectionist and she doesn't like me, but we get along. I let her think she's killing me with her tales of doglike devotion from you. Works like a charm.''

He didn't like that. "Doglike devotion isn't what she gets from me."

"Oh, I know what she does get from you. She tells me *that*, too,'' she added, and this time she couldn't keep the sting it caused out of her face.

"There isn't anything to tell,'' he said through his teeth. "I'm not sleeping with her!''

She shrugged with majestic acting ability. "Don't deprive yourself on my account,'' she said carelessly. "I'm certainly not nursing any hopes in that direction. When I marry, and I will someday, my husband is going to be my first lover.''

His pride felt as if she'd lanced it. His face felt hot as he glared down at her. "He'll have to be something special, to settle for a virginal wife these days,'' he said icily, striking out.

"Maybe he'll think he's blessed,'' she countered, refusing to allow his words to bother her. "It takes an intelligent woman not to risk her health and her future husband's for the sake of not standing out in a crowd."

"You puritan," he accused coldly.

"My morals are my own affair, and none of your business. You're just the security chief for my company!"

His dark eyes slid over hers. "Try again."

"You have no right to... Oh!"

He pulled her close in his arms, and his mouth was hard and hungry over her soft lips. She stiffened and tried to reject him, but his arms only closed more firmly, enveloping her against his big, powerful body while his mouth nudged and coaxed and teased until her lips finally parted.

Even then, he didn't take immediate advantage of it. His open mouth brushed lazily over hers, tormenting it until she moaned and began pushing upward, trying to capture his elusive mouth against her own. It was yesterday, and she was in love and aching for Lang, all over again.

"Tell me what you want," he coaxed. His hands were on her hips, now, pulling and dragging them against the hard male thrust of him, so that she could feel the evidence of his need.

"Lang." She choked out his name.

"Come on," he said, daring her, "tell me what you want me to do, Kirry."

"Not... fair," she stammered.

"Is life?" His hand slid into the thick short hair at her nape and contracted, tilting her face at just the angle he wanted. His eyes were vaguely frightening as they glittered down into hers. "Now," he breathed, lowering his head, "now, open your mouth and taste me inside, and let me taste you. Make me forget..."

She felt his mouth, warm and moist, burrowing slowly into her own. The contact with his body, the strength of his arms, took her own strength away. She yielded, melting into him, unmindful of the past or the future while she savored the intimate touch of his tongue sliding into her mouth.

The erotic symbolism of the caress made her body go taut with sudden desire. She shivered, and he laughed, then deepened the kiss with a slow, teasing rhythm.

Knots coiled in her lower belly. Her legs trembled helplessly and she moaned as the fever burned higher between them.

His other hand dropped to the very base of her spine and began to move her against him. She made a sound that went right up his backbone, and his mouth echoed it in the stillness of the hallway.

Only the steady hum of the elevator broke them apart. He stepped back from her just as an elderly couple got off the conveyance, glanced toward them indulgently and walked hand in hand down the other end of the hall to their own apartment.

Lang felt too drained to move. He heard the door close in the distance and only then did he look at Kirry. She seemed to be as devastated as he. She was leaning back against her own door, and her soft mouth was swollen and red from his kisses.

"I could have you right now," he said. His voice was deep with feeling. "You know it, too."

"Let's not forget Lorna," she said through the maelstrom of emotions that were buffeting her mind.

"Damn Lorna! I want you!"

She had to drag her eyes away from his. "You've overheated, that's all," she said stiffly. "A nice cold shower should fix you right up."

"Lorna wouldn't send me into a shower," he said in a soft, threatening tone.

Her eyes narrowed. "Then why don't you go and see her, dear man?"

Her lack of cooperation made him furious. "Thanks for the suggestion," he said. "I might do fhat."

He whirled on his heel, in a furious temper, and stalked to the elevator. He jabbed the Down button furiously, and as if the elevator knew his mood, it appeared promptly from the floor above. He got into it without even darting a glance at Kirry.

She could have screamed. She wasn't going to go to bed with him just to keep him away from Lorna, and if he thought she was, he still didn't know her very well.

She unlocked the door and slammed it firmly behind her. How could he! Why had he kissed her in the first place? Now she was going to toss and turn all night, sickened by images of Lorna nude in his big arms in bed. She hated him! How in the world had she ever imagined that she could love someone as cruel as Lang? She was going to have to get herself together.

Lang was no longer her concern. The sooner she realized it, the better.

Lang, meanwhile, was driving aimlessly around town, and nowhere near Lorna's apartment. He should never have touched Kirry that way. Now he was going to spend hours remembering her soft warmth in his arms, the hunger in her kisses. She wanted him; she couldn't hide it.

But he'd let her throw him off-balance with those stinging comments she made. She was jealous of Lorna and afraid to trust him. That was the crux of the matter. He'd just have to learn to keep his temper and try harder. But meanwhile, there was Erikson to deal with. The gas grenade had shaken Lang as much as it had Kirry. He had to do something about Erikson while there was still time.

The next morning, Lang was more cautious than ever. He buzzed Kirry's doorbell thirty minutes before she was due at work. She dragged herself out of bed in her short nightie and looked through the peephole before she reluctantly opened the door.

"Don't stare," she told him irritably, her hair tousled from sleep, her green eyes half-closed with it. "I'm not a peep show."

"Darlin', I never said you were," he drawled, smiling at the exquisite tanned length of her legs and the soft thrust of her breasts against the thin fabric. She had a devastating figure. "But in that rig, you could turn a blind man's head."

"I don't want to turn your head. I just want to get dressed and go to work. There's some coffee in the kitchen. You can drink it while I get changed."

"You're sure you wouldn't like to go in like that?" he asked, smiling at the pleasure she gave him in the skimpy outfit.

She put her hands on her rounded hips and glowered at him. "It's only a body. Lorna has one just like it, as I'm sure you found out all over again last night!"

His eyebrows lifted and he smiled. "Jealous?"

"Of Lorna? Hah! Why should I be jealous? I don't want you!"

"You did last night," he reminded her.

"I won't dignify that statement with an answer. And I did not want you!" She whirled and went into the bedroom, pushing the door almost shut. She stripped off the nightie and was standing there in her lacy pink bikini briefs, fuming with bad temper, when the door opened and Lang's eyes froze on her body.

Seven

Kirry couldn't even breathe. The way Lang was looking at her made her go hot all over.

"Don't panic and start leaping for cover," he said quietly. He put his hands into his pockets and leaned back against the door facing. "I can't help staring— you're unbelievably pretty like that—but I promise I won't touch until you want me to."

She felt hot and cold all over, and there were swellings in her body that were familiar, left from the days when Lang made soft, slow love to her without ever crossing the line.

She should get dressed, she told herself. She was brazen, standing there with her body open to him, letting him look. Oh, but it was sweet to feel his eyes! They made her throb with forbidden pleasures.

He saw the need in her face, in the faint trembling of her legs. With a soft sound in the back of his throat, he jerked away from the door and moved toward her.

Run, her mind said. But her legs wouldn't work. He came closer, filling the room, filling her hungry eyes.

He still didn't touch her. He searched her face in silence. After a minute, a soft smile flamed on his mouth. His hand went to his tie and slowly unfastened it. He tossed it aside. He slid out of his jacket, and it followed the tie into a chair, while Kirry shivered at what she saw in his face.

"I don't...want to...now," she whispered when his hands went to his shirt. But she still wasn't moving.

"Neither do I," he replied quietly. "But some things are fated, I suppose."

His shirt was unbuttoned, removed, baring a broad, bronzed chest thick with black, curling hair. He brought her hands to his belt.

"Take it off," he whispered.

Her hands trembled on the buckle and her wide eyes sought his for reassurance.

"I'll take care of you. We won't take risks," he said, reading the apprehension. He saw her relax, despite the traces of guilt that remained in her soft green eyes. He bent and brushed his mouth over her closing eyelids, hiding the accusation in them. "I'll take a long time," he whispered. "Do you trust me not to hurt you?"

She moved closer, drawn like a magnet to the feel of his hair-roughened chest against her bare breasts. She shivered as the nipples went hard when she pushed into him and let her arms encircle his waist. "I trust you," she stated.

He let out a savage breath. He hadn't dreamed that it would happen like this. Years of wanting her, waiting, hoping . . . And she was giving in, without a single protest.

The stillness in the bedroom was haunting. Above it, he could hear faint street noises in the distance. Closer, he could hear Kirry's tortured breathing, feel the warmth of it against his chest where her lips touched.

"Will you hate me?" he asked heavily.

She lifted her misty eyes to his. "Will you think I'm cheap?" she asked with equal concern.

He smiled. "You?" he whispered tenderly.

She pressed closer, resting her cheek against his warm chest. She clung, trembling, as the finality of it trespassed into her mind.

His big hands smoothed over her bare back, savoring its silkiness. "There's a condition," he said through a tight throat.

"What?"

"Afterward, you have to put the ring back on."

Her eyes opened. She could see the heavy vibration of his chest. "The ring?"

His mouth brushed hungrily against her hair and his hands pulled her closer. "The engagement ring, Kirry," he whispered, and his mouth quickly worked its way down her flushed face to her mouth. He took it hungrily and felt it open, felt her body quicken even as he heard her helpless moan of pleasure.

He interpreted her response as an agreement, a sacred oath. After that, nothing on earth would have stopped him.

He lifted her, his mouth still covering hers, and carried her to the bed.

She looked up as he laid her gently on the covers. "Are you going to close . . . close the bedroom door?"

"Who's going to see us, my darling?" he whispered. He slid down beside her, letting his eyes caress the soft thrust of her breasts before his mouth lowered to tease and torment them into rigid peaks.

Kirry couldn't have imagined the pleasure. It was frantic, all-consuming. She let him remove the final barrier and then lay trembling, watching him with hungry eyes while he undressed for her. She'd never seen him totally nude. She looked at him now without embarrassment, glorying in the perfection of his powerful body.

He lowered himself against her, smiling at her expression. "We can't have secrets anymore, can we?" he asked gently. His mouth touched hers, and then roamed over her face while his hands began to learn her with infinite patience and tender caresses. He felt her tremble, heard her soft gasps as he went from one intimacy to another in the rapt silence.

She'd never imagined making love in broad daylight. Now it seemed natural, perfect. She led where he followed, awash in pleasure so intense that she had no control left when he finally paused for a moment to protect her, and then moved down. She felt his body slowly invade hers and she shivered, her hands clutching with anticipation and a little fear.

His mouth was at her ear, his breath hot and quick. His tongue teased inside her ear. His hand slid down her belly and he touched her, laughing with intimate tenderness when she gasped and her hips arched up to accommodate him.

"Lang!" she cried out.

"Yes, isn't it shocking?" he breathed with joyful conspiracy. "Shocking, earthy..." He pushed down and heard the breath leave her body. "And now you know it all, don't you?" he whispered, as he possessed her completely. "You know me. All of me. And I know all... of... you."

His body was moving. She felt him around her, within her, felt a tension that made her reach up to him, move with him, searching for the right pressure, the right rhythm. She swallowed, gasping. She felt the heat and dampness of him with wonder. She heard his rough breath at her ear, felt his control give way at last.

His lean hand gripped her thigh and the rhythm grew ruthless. She was beyond caring about how he held her. It was there, the pleasure was there, and she was... about... to touch it...!

She was sobbing. She heard her own voice with a sense of disassociation, as if she was no longer in her body at all, but sailing around with Lang in a miasma of golden heat and throbbing satisfaction. She cried out something and arched her back to prolong the exquisite sensations that rippled over her in waves of pleasure.

For a few seconds, there was nothing else in the world except Lang, who had become completely part of her.

Far away, she heard ragged breathing and felt a crushing weight the length of her body. She opened her eyes. The ceiling was there, with the sunlight reflecting on the light fixture. She moved her fingers experimentally and felt the cold silk of Lang's thick hair. She remembered then, and smiled.

He felt the smile against his cheek and lifted his head. His eyes, like hers, were soft in the aftermath of fulfillment. He lifted himself enough to see her face and smiled back.

Her body began to throb all over again. He hadn't moved away and when she shifted one leg, she felt him intimately. His eyes grew misty with the return of desire, like her own.

He moved, too, and watched her lips part.

She reached up, arching her hips so that she caressed him in the most exciting way, and he reacted with incredible ease. His breath caught at the quickening.

"That's impossible," she assured him. "I read it in a book...."

"Written by a virgin, no doubt," he breathed into her open mouth, and began to move again.

"Lang...isn't it risky...?"

He stilled. "Yes." He bit off the word. "My God, yes!" With anguish in his face, he lifted away from her, and fell onto his back. He lay there, his fists clenched, totally vulnerable while he fought to still the demons.

She leaned over him, boldly watching his face while he struggled with the desire he didn't dare satisfy. His eyes held hers while he forced himself to breathe normally until the pain subsided. His gaze slid down to her soft breasts and lingered there. He pulled her closer and kissed them hungrily.

"I want to do it again and again and again," she whispered softly, savoring his mouth on her body.

"So do I. But I don't want to make a baby in the fever of it," he whispered back. He held her close then, while they slowly came down from the heights.

She closed her eyes and went heavy against him, gloriously contented. "Do you really want to marry me?" she asked daringly.

"Yes," he said.

She drew her cheek against his chest, and the clean scent of him came up into her nostrils. "When?"

"We can talk about dates later," he murmured, oddly reluctant to pin it down to a certainty. He smoothed her hair. "We have to get to work."

She lifted herself to look at the clock and groaned. "Oh, my goodness, I'm an hour late!"

"The world won't end," he murmured dryly.

"That's what you think! I have a business meeting in a half hour!"

"Look at me."

She did, and his smile was her undoing. "Don't panic," he said. "I'll get you there in time."

He kissed her gently and put her out of the bed, stretching lazily as he got to his feet. "Come on. We'll have time for a quick shower."

He led her into the bathroom and put her into the shower with him. It took longer than it normally would, because he made her bathe him and that led to exploration and soft kisses that made him grit his teeth.

"I'm not prepared." He chuckled, lifting her out of the spray. He turned the shower off and dried her. "No accidents."

His concern seemed rather beyond what she might have expected. She felt insecure. "I'll see the doctor," she promised, "so that we can make sure nothing happens until we want it to."

He studied her rapt face quietly. "Your career means a lot to you, doesn't it?" he asked solemnly. "For now, at least?"

She read the thoughts in his face. "Yes," she said slowly. She frowned. "You...do eventually want a child?"

He smiled, but it didn't reach his eyes. "Of course I do. Now, let's get to work. Tonight, we'll drive down to Floresville and tell Bob and Connie our good news."

She wanted to pin him down on the subject of a family. Perhaps he was just thinking of her. But there had been something in his eyes when she mentioned children....

He smoothed down the frown. "Stop borrowing trouble and get dressed. Just look what you've made me do," he said, glowering. "I've been seduced, for God's sake!"

Her eyes twinkled. "Why, so you have. Would you like to press charges?"

"I'd like to press something," he murmured, chuckling.

"I did offer," she reminded him.

He bent and kissed her carelessly. "I'll be prepared next time."

"Or I will," she added.

While Lang gathered his own clothes and began to dress, she moved to her dresser and pulled out a bra and slip and quickly put them on with her back to Lang. Feeling a little shy now, she walked to the closet and took out a green, patterned shirtwaist dress and put it on.

"You look nice in green," he said.

"Thanks." She hesitated, suddenly remembering his abrupt arrival. "Why did you come by this morning?" she asked.

"I'm giving you a ride into work. And I wanted to know if you got any calls last night," he said with a lazy smile.

She smiled back and shook her head. "There was nothing on the answering machine. Nobody bothered me at all. Is this some new tactic he's using?" she asked then. "Is he trying to drive me crazy by waiting several days between incidents?"

"It's a good psychological trick," he agreed. "I wouldn't put it past him. But that gas grenade was dangerous. Sometimes they start fires. If it had been beneath the seat, and it had exploded under you..."

"I get the message," she said uneasily. Her eyes met his in the mirror while she put on makeup and ran a comb through her short hair. "In other words, we're not out of the woods yet."

He nodded.

She put down the brush and searched in another drawer for her panty hose. She put them on while Lang watched with appreciative eyes, then she slipped on her high heels and picked up her purse.

"What about my car?" she asked. "You didn't get it picked up, did you?"

He shook his head. "Sorry. I'll see to it this morning."

She turned and looked at him blatantly. "Did you see Lorna last night?" she asked slowly.

He lifted an amused eyebrow. "If I had, do you think I'd have been so hungry for you?"

She flushed. "Well..."

He drew her against him. "You still don't know much. Some men can go all night. I can't. If I'd been with another woman all night, I wouldn't have been capable this morning. Does that answer the question you can't quite ask me?"

"Yes," she said ruefully. "Sorry, I shouldn't have pried."

He frowned. "Kirry, you trusted me enough to let me make love to you," he reminded her softly. "That gives you every right in the world to know about me. I haven't slept with Lorna, and I won't. I want to marry you."

He said he did. But he wouldn't talk about a date and he didn't want to risk making her pregnant. She almost mentioned that, but what they'd shared was too new and exciting to spoil. She decided to live one day at a time. At least he did want her for keeps this time. She could settle for that. For now.

She reached up and kissed him very softly. Her eyes adored him. She tried not to notice the indecision in his. "Let's go see if we're fired," she teased, and stepped away from him.

"Right."

He drove her to the office in a faintly strained silence. He'd burned his bridges this time. There would be no going back. He'd compromised her, and as old-fashioned as it might seem to another modern man, he felt obliged to do the right thing and marry her. He did care about her, very much. It was just that he was trapped now. It didn't feel as comfortable as he'd thought it would, to be totally committed. And she wanted children.

He loved Mikey, of course, but it would be different when the child was his own, and he became responsible for it and Kirry. She was a working woman. She wanted a career. But she'd slept with him, and now his old footloose days were gone forever, because he hadn't been able to hold back. He'd wanted Kirry to the point of madness. He glanced at her, remembering how it had been, and he couldn't manage to regret that heated loving in her bed. No matter what the cost, it was worth it! He only had to get used to the idea of being committed. That shouldn't be so hard, he told himself firmly. He'd gotten used to being on the road all the time when he joined the Company, he'd gotten used to wearing a gun. He'd even managed to live with worse things. It would grow on him. And as for children, he'd find some way to put her off. With that certainty in mind, he smiled at Kirry and broke into casual conversation.

But she wasn't fooled. She saw the worry on his face, the indecision he couldn't hide. He'd gone over the edge with her and now he was sorry about it, she could tell. He was going to make the best of it, but how was she going to be able to live with a man who was forcing himself to act contented? It was a glimpse of a nightmare.

The one nice thing about the morning was that Erickson was nowhere in sight, in either of his cars. But she'd been overly relieved one time too many, so she wasn't taking anything for granted. He might be hiding nearby, waiting for her to relax.

Lang stopped the car at her office door and turned to her. "Don't let your guard down," he said gently. "Just because we don't see him doesn't mean that he isn't around."

"I was just thinking the same thing," she replied. Her eyes searched his. "I'm sorry," she said gently.

He frowned. "About what?"

She shrugged a thin shoulder and forced a smile. "You aren't ready," she said. "You thought you were, but you aren't. I was as much to blame as you were for what happened, so you don't need to feel guilty. You don't need to feel obligated to marry me, either. We were careful. There won't be any...consequences."

He stared at her with conflicting emotions. "Are you sure you don't want to marry me, Kirry?" he asked slowly.

The way he phrased it said everything. She didn't dare cry or look regretful. "I enjoyed what we did," she said. "But when the newness wore off, we'd still be stuck with each other. You have your job and I have mine, and marriage isn't the end of the rainbow anymore. Maybe we 'd better think about this before we jump into it."

"That's exactly how I feel," he said, and looked relieved. "But we can still be engaged, while we're thinking about it. Okay?"

Wimp, she told herself. "Okay," she agreed too readily, and then grimaced at her own scramble for crumbs.

"We can drive down and have supper with Connie and Bob. I'll call them."

"I'd enjoy seeing them again."

"I'll pick you up here after work. Be careful."

She nodded, hesitating weakly.

His eyes began to glitter. "Want me to kiss you?" he murmured, teasing.

She started to deny it, but the irony of the situation made her smile. "Yes," she said.

He smiled. "I like that honesty," he said, his voice husky and deep. "I want to kiss you, too."

She moved closer and tilted her face up for him. He framed it in his big hands and bent, drawing his lips softly over her own. But the passion between them was too raw and new to allow for tenderness just yet, and very quickly, he had her close in his arms and was kissing the breath out of her. She moaned, and he came to his senses.

"I can't take much of that," he said with graveyard humor. He took out his handkerchief and removed the smeared lipstick from around her mouth and then his own. "I'll come by and take you out to lunch, if you're free."

"I'm not," she said miserably. "I have to meet some of Lorna's group for a business lunch."

He sighed. "Okay. Another time."

She nodded, reaching for the door.

He stayed her hand. "I haven't given Lorna any messages for you," he said quietly. "If she starts handing out tidbits about me, take them with a grain of salt, will you?"

She smiled over her shoulder. "Okay."

"I'll see you later."

"Sure." She got out and walked into the building, and had to force herself not to look back. She'd made her bed. Now she was going to have to lie in it.

"You're late," Mack grumbled the minute she walked in the door. "Lorna McLane has been on the phone ten times asking where you were. She couldn't seem to locate our security chief, either." He looked at Kirry suspiciously. "Do you know where he is?"

"He was with me," she said, fighting a blush.

Mack hesitated. "Oh."

"You needn't look so shocked. Lang and I are engaged," she added.

His face relaxed into a beaming smile. "Congratulations."

"Those might be a little premature. We're not planning an elopement."

"You never know," he replied. "Lang strikes me as an impulsive man."

"He strikes most people that way. But he's actually very cautious," she said, remembering him with the familiarity of years. "He's very methodical. He always thinks first."

She remembered that when she was alone in her office. Lang was extremely cautious, in fact. He never leaped before he looked, or let his emotions lead him around. So why had he let himself go with her this morning? Despite the fact that he took precautions, it was totally unlike him to leap in without considering the consequences. At the very least, Kirry's feelings for him would lead her to expect commitment from a man who seduced her. He knew that. Had he really lost his head? Or had he changed enough that he might actually want to marry her?

She didn't have time to ponder the question for very long. Lorna McLane called again, and she was fuming.

"Where have you been, Miss Campbell?" she asked in a scathing tone. "I really don't have all day to chase you down. Do you want this account or not?"

Kirry bit her tongue to keep from telling the truth. "Certainly we want it, Miss McLane," she said in a pacifying tone. "I'm sorry, I was unavoidably detained getting to work this morning."

"By Lang?" came the poisonous reply.

Kirry's hand tightened on the receiver. "If you must know, yes," she replied curtly.

"You little tramp," Lorna said huskily.

"Lang and I are engaged to be married, Miss McLane," Kirry informed her. "What we do in our private lives is hardly any of your business!"

There was an indrawn breath and a long pause, with audible breathing. "He wouldn't... he isn't the marrying kind! You're lying!"

"If you think so, you're at liberty to ask him."

"I've called him a number of times, but he's never around. I guess he's been with you."

"I've had some problems here. Lang has been teaching me self-defense," she returned.

"And a few other tricks, I'll bet. He's a wonderful lover, isn't he?" she drawled. "But wait until you get him to the altar before you start looking for congratulations. He was engaged to me, once, too. He doesn't want children, did you know?" she added with a poisonous note in her voice. "He has to be free to walk out if he wants to, so kids are out of the question."

"He wants children. We both do," she said hesitantly.

"Really? Pin him down, dear. I dare you."

"Miss McLane, this is really..."

"I'll expect to see you at lunch," Lorna continued unabashed. "I've asked the Lancasters to join us while we discuss the details of this promotion. I would really prefer to have your colleague, Mack, work on it. I find that women aren't quite as cooperative as men when I make suggestions."

I'm not surprised, Kirry thought, but she didn't dare say it. She was trying to picture Miss McLane wrapped from toes to eyes in green satin and pinned with safety pins. It kept her sane.

"I'm sure I'd have no objections to Mack replacing me," Kirry volunteered, thinking that Mack would kill her for stepping down. He had no affection for Lorna.

"Then, we'll be able to settle this amicably. I'm so glad."

"I'll see you at lunch, then."

"Indeed you will," Lorna purred, and made it sound like a threat.

Eight

Lorna had a surprise for Kirry at lunch. Not only had she insisted that the Lancasters be in attendance, but Lang was there, too, looking irritable and reluctant.

"I'm sure you won't mind if Lang joins us," Lorna told Kirry privately. "I thought you might like the Lancasters to share in the news of your engagement."

She moved away in a cloud of expensive perfume to greet the dark, elegantly dressed Lancasters before Kirry could reply. "I know that I won't be giving away any terrible secrets if I tell you that Lang and Miss Campbell are to be married," Lorna told the Lancasters, smiling.

Kirry wanted to tell her that feathers were sticking out of her mouth, but she didn't dare. She smiled instead, although she couldn't keep it from looking strained.

"Is this true?" Mrs. Lancaster asked, delighted.

Lang straightened. He glared at Lorna and moved closer to Kirry, taking her hand in his. "Yes, it is," he said, but he didn't sound like a happy bridegroom.

"Well, we must help with the arrangements for the wedding," Mrs. Lancaster continued, and her husband smiled his agreement. "When is it to be?"

"We haven't set a date," Lang said stiffly.

"Surely you plan to make it soon, Lang, dear?" Lorna mused, leaning back to smile at him with hatred in her eyes.

"There's no rush," he said firmly. "Kirry and I have plenty of time."

Kirry knew that he didn't like to be pushed, but there was more to it than that. He was so obviously reluctant to be pinned down on a date that it was embarrassing.

"That's right," Kirry said quickly, backing him up only because she didn't like Lorna. "We plan on a long engagement."

"I see," Mr. Lancaster replied with narrowed eyes.

"Well, if you're not planning to start a family right away, I suppose there's no hurry about it," Lorna purred. "How many children are you going to have, Lang?" she asked. "Two or three?"

Lang's face went rigid. "We haven't discussed that."

"Surely you want a son?" Lorna persisted.

He glared at her and then deliberately glanced at his watch.

"We'd better get started," Mr. Lancaster said, taking the hint. "We all have duties to perform. Now what is this about switching the service on your account, Miss McLane?" he asked politely.

"It's nothing against Miss Campbell," Lorna assured him, "but I think Mack would be more... accessible. I've spent the entire morning trying to track down Miss Campbell, who seems to be celebrating her engagement with a little, shall we say, excessive enthusiasm? You know how the job can suffer when people have their heads in the clouds," she added with a silvery little laugh.

Why, you vicious shrew, Kirry was thinking. In one stroke, Lorna had managed to make her look like an incompetent airhead.

"I was late to work, yes," Kirry said angrily. "But it was hardly dereliction of duty...!"

"Miss Campbell," Mr. Lancaster said sharply, and smiled pointedly. "We wouldn't want to alienate Miss McLane, now, would we?"

Kirry flushed. "Excuse me. I'm sorry that I wasn't available this morning, and I can assure you that in the future..."

"In the future, I would prefer to deal with Mack," she said, smiling at her warmly. "He and I will get along very well. And this account is *so* important...." She let her voice trail away.

Kirry was being railroaded, and the Lancasters were taking it all in without question. Mrs. Lancaster's friendship with Lorna obviously inclined her to believe whatever the former model told her. She gave Kirry a speaking glance.

"Indeed the account is important," Mrs. Lancaster said coolly. "I'm sure that Miss Campbell won't mind letting Mack take it over."

The inference was that she'd better *not* mind. Kirry was losing ground and she didn't know how to regain it.

"Of course I don't mind," she said diplomatically. "Miss McLane's satisfaction must be our first priority."

Lorna inclined her head graciously. "I'm delighted that you're willing to cooperate. Heaven forbid that I should cause any trouble. But this promotion must be perfect. And it will lead to others. I have many connections in the fashion industry."

"I'm aware of that, my dear," Mrs. Lancaster said brightly. "Your influence is far-reaching, indeed."

Mr. Lancaster was watching Kirry closely. "You have other accounts to service, I presume?" he asked her curtly. It was the first time he'd taken any real interest in what she did for his company.

"I've been working on a promotional campaign for a new chain of soup and salad bars," Kirry told him. "The first television ad runs tonight, in fact, at eight."

"We'll be sure to watch," he informed her.

Kirry was confident that the campaign would be successful, and she wasn't worried, despite the faint threat in Lancaster's voice. She was obviously on trial now, thanks to Lorna's dirty work, but she wouldn't cower. She held her head up through the rest of the meeting and smiled as if she hadn't a care in the world.

"I hope I'll be invited to the wedding," Lorna told Lang as the meeting broke up. "And the first christening, of course."

Lang didn't smile. "That was a low thing to do," he said quietly. "Whatever vendettas you have against me shouldn't extend to Kirry. She's never done anything to hurt you."

"No?" Lorna's eyes glittered. "She took you away from me, didn't she?"

"No woman can take a man who isn't willing," he informed her. "You and I are water and wax. We're too different to make a pair."

"You wanted me!" she accused.

He nodded. "You were an important part of my life for a while. I hope I was as important to you. But I never told you any lies, or made any promises, and you damned well know it."

She was barely in control of her temper. She glanced at Kirry, talking to Mrs. Lancaster, and took a sharp breath. "She looks slept with," she said bluntly, looking up in time to catch Lang's expression. "So that's it. Poor little compromised virgin. Did you feel obligated to offer her marriage in exchange, Lang?" she asked.

"How interesting. Do you know what sort of people the Lancasters are? They're fundamentalists."

"Are you making threats, Lorna?" he asked.

"Why, yes, I am," she said with a smile. "Either you break that engagement or I'll give the Lancasters an earful about her lack of morals. And when I get through, she won't have a job...or a reference. You do know what I mean, don't you, dear?"

She walked away, smiling. Lang stared after her with murderous eyes. He hadn't dreamed that she could be so spiteful. He'd taken her out to make Kirry jealous, but he hadn't done it in any spiteful or obvious way. For all Lorna knew, he was simply renewing an old acquaintance. Only Lorna had taken it seriously, and she wanted to play for keeps. Now Lang was between a rock and a hard place. Either he had to marry Kirry immediately or give her up, because if Lorna carried through with her threat, Kirry would literally be asked to sacrifice her career. Her job meant a lot to her. He knew too well how much careers mattered to some women....

"You're very quiet," Kirry remarked when they were on the way down to Bob and Connie's house in Floresville. "What's wrong?"

He glanced at her and back at the road. "Just thinking. Have you seen anything of Erikson today?"

She shook her head and wrapped her arms tightly around her chest, leaning back in the seat with a shiver. "Could you turn up the heat, Lang?"

"Sure." He frowned. "You aren't catching a cold, are you?"

She shook her head. "I'm just tired and worried. The Lancasters didn't like what Lorna said at lunch, I know they didn't. What if they think I'm too incompetent to keep on?"

"Aren't you good at your job?"

"Well, yes, but so are a lot of other people. I'm original, at least. Which is more than I can say for poor old Mack," she said, grimacing. "He doesn't like Lorna and he hates high fashion. He finds it boring. He's not going to do a job she'll like."

"What did you have in mind?" he asked, smiling.

"A star-studded extravaganza with some socialites helping to model Lorna's clothing line," she said. "They'd not only love the limelight, they'd buy the clothes. It would mean quick sales and a lot more than just surface promotion. At least one local debutante has a father who owns a network of boutiques internationallly. Even Lorna doesn't have connections like that." She shrugged. "But she's not interested in my ideas. I tried to show her what I had in mind, and she just ignored me. She wouldn't even listen."

"Pity she doesn't have any competition," he mused. "You could put her nose in a sling."

"She does have competition," she remarked. "But they're represented by another company and as far as I know, they don't have any promotions planned for the rest of the year."

He gave her a lingering look at a traffic light. "There is such a thing as taking the bit between the teeth. Why don't you go to the competition and outline your ideas and offer to take the thing on as an independent promoter?"

She gasped. "That would be unethical."

"Give your notice at Lancaster. Change jobs. Gamble."

"Lang, I have bills to pay," she exclaimed with a surprised laugh. "I can't take a chance like that. I'm not a gambler."

"I'm not, either, as a rule. But sometimes you have to take a chance."

"You don't take chances."

"No? I asked you to marry me."

She averted her eyes and stared out the window with a sinking heart.

"That was badly put, wasn't it?" he asked quietly. "I'm sorry. I was trying to cheer you up."

"Lorna saw right through you today," she said. "She pushed you into a corner and as much as made you admit that you didn't want to marry me."

His hand tightened on the steering wheel as he was forced to remember the threat Lorna had made.

"I admitted nothing."

She turned in her seat, adjusting her seat belt, and studied his profile. "You aren't ready," she said simply. "To you, commitment is still the boogeyman. You think of marriage as a sort of prison, with children as the chains that keep people there."

He winced. "Kirry..."

She touched his sleeve, feeling the warm strength of his arm under it. "We can be engaged for a little while, until I make up my mind what I'm going to do—stay with the agency or take that chance and go independent. But I won't take the engagement seriously, and I don't want you to. Your conscience may sting for a while about what we did, but you'll get over it. Nothing happened, Lang. We just made love. People do it all the time. No big deal."

"It was to me," he said shortly, glowering down at her. "And if it was no big deal, why haven't you done it before now with some other man?"

She leaned her head against the seat and looked at him quietly. "You know why. You've always known. It's because I belong to you."

His heart shivered in his chest. He couldn't look at her again. She was tying him in knots, but they were of his own making. He didn't want her to belong to him. He didn't want to be a prisoner of his conscience or even of love.

She withdrew her hand and looked out the windshield. She'd embarrassed him. At the very least, she'd made him uncomfortable. "Don't torture yourself," she said quietly. "I'm not asking for anything."

"I know that," he said tersely.

She closed her eyes, enjoying the company and the darkness as they sped toward Floresville. If only they could keep driving forever, she thought. It would be lovely not to have to go back to all her problems and the future, when Lang would be out of her life again, and forever this time.

She was dreaming. Lang had made love to her, and they were sprawled under a big oak tree by a beautiful stream in a meadow, holding each other. He was whispering how much he loved her...

"Will you wake up?" he demanded curtly, shaking her. "We're here, and all hell has broken loose from the sound of things!"

She sat up, her dream shattered by his harsh tone. "What?" she asked, confused.

"Listen!"

The car was sitting in the driveway of the old Victorian house where the Pattons lived. A loud voice—Bob's—was disclaiming some accusation that came from Connie. In the background, a soft Spanish voice was trying to assert reason.

"Housekeeper, my blue elbow! You were kissing her!" Connie was raging.

"I was holding her while she cried, because you hurt her feelings!" Bob yelled. All three of them were outlined on the front porch. "You didn't have to accuse her of being a homewrecker!"

"Well, she is!" Connie said. "She's even taken over Mikey! He wants Teresa to read to him, he wants Teresa to take him to school, he wants Teresa to sit by him when we eat...he's *my* son!"

"He'd never know it, would he, when you've got your nose stuck in engines all day and half the night!"

"Oh!" Connie threw up her hands and started to say something else when she noticed the car in the driveway. She smoothed down her greasy coveralls and glanced from the car to Bob.

"Lang!" his brother exclaimed, grateful for the diversion. "Lang, is that you?"

"Looks like it," Lang said ruefully. He got out and waited for Kirry to join him at the steps. "We just got engaged and thought we'd come and tell you. This doesn't look like the best time for an announcement."

"Engaged?" Connie stumbled. "You and Kirry? Again?"

"We weren't actually engaged then," Lang said irritably. "We were almost engaged."

Connie's face softened. "Well, well. And when are you getting married, soon?"

"I wish everybody would stop asking that!" Lang burst out, running an irritated big hand through his hair.

"We haven't set a date," Kirry said quickly. "It was very sudden. We haven't really had a lot of time to talk about it, what with our jobs..."

"Well, of course they haven't," Bob told his wife. "Can't you stop throwing questions at them when they've only just gotten here? Teresa, make some coffee and slice some cake, will you?!"

"*Si*, Señor Bob," Teresa's soft voice came back, followed by the scurrying of feet.

"She's a sweetheart," Bob said with a smile. It faded when he looked at his haggard wife. "She doesn't think so. She doesn't even appreciate all the hard work Teresa does here to save her work."

"I'm sure Connie appreciates it, Bob," Kirry interjected. "Can we go inside? I'm cold."

"It's all but summer," Lang muttered. "How can you have chills?"

"Are you feverish?" Connie felt Kirry's forehead. "Not at all, thank goodness. You know, I had chills when I got pregnant with Mikey..."

"There's no possibility whatsoever that Kirry's pregnant," Lang said shortly.

"Oh, I know that, for heaven's sake," Connie muttered at him. "I was just making a statement."

Lang flushed, but no one noticed except Kirry. She averted her eyes. They'd taken precautions, and it had only been the one time. She couldn't be pregnant. The thing was, precautions did fail one time out of a hundred.... But, no, she wouldn't think about it.

"This is Teresa." Bob introduced the young Mexican-American woman with a smile. His eyes were twinkling as he looked at her. "*Ninita, éste es mi hermano,* Lang."

"*Mucho gusto enconocerlo, señor,*" she said with a smile. She had a lovely round figure and big brown eyes in a frame of long, jet black hair. She was a beauty. No wonder Connie was furious!

"*Y mi,*" Lang replied. "*Se alegro de trabajar aquí, señorita?*" he added.

"Oh, sí," she said without enthusiasm, and she looked worried. *"Éste familia es muy simpático, especialamente el ninito."*

She liked Mikey. She didn't mention liking Connie, who was glaring at everybody who spoke Spanish, because she didn't.

"Speak English," Connie said harshly.

"She's learning. It takes time." Bob shot back the words. "Stop being so unpleasant!"

Connie put her hands on her hips and glared at him. "I will not. You're imagining yourself in love with her, aren't you?"

Bob flushed. "For heaven's sake . . . !"

"Admit it, you coward!" Connie goaded him. "Come on, admit it!"

"She's a sweet, kind little thing who likes kids and housework and men!" he said finally, his dark eyes glaring at her. "How do you expect me to feel about her, when my wife looks and smells like a grease pit and never has time for me or her son?"

Connie gasped and suddenly turned and ran for the bedroom, where she slammed the door with a loud sob.

Bob grimaced. "Now I've done it."

Lang and Kirry exchanged looks. "I think we picked a bad night to come," Lang began.

"There aren't any good ones," he muttered. He saw Teresa's huge eyes fill with tears and moved to put an arm around her. *"No sea triste, amada,"* he said softly. *"Todo es bien."*

"Everything is not well," Lang replied darkly. "And she should be sad, since it seems to me that she's about to break up your marriage. You're a married man, Bob. Why don't you act like it? The person who needs comforting is your wife, not your housekeeper."

Bob's face flamed. He took his arm from around Teresa and glowered at Lang. "I don't need you to tell me how to conduct my marriage!"

"No?" Lang looked past him. Connie was coming out of the bedroom with a suitcase in one hand and Mikey by the other.

"Where are we going, Mom?" he asked sleepily.

"To my sister's!" she informed the world. She glared at Bob. "When you come to your senses, if you do, I'll be at Louise's."

"What about your precious business out back?" he asked.

"Put up a Closed sign. You can spell that, can't you?" she asked sweetly. "In the meanwhile, Todd Steele has a vacancy for a mechanic in his garage, and he'll hire me in a minute."

His eyes bulged. "I won't have you working for your ex-sweetheart who just got divorced!" he told her.

"Why not? I'm about to be divorced myself!"

"Connie!" he wailed.

"Mom, why are you yelling at my daddy?" Mikey asked, still drowsy and not making much sense of the confrontation.

"Because he's deaf," Connie replied, glaring at her husband. "He doesn't understand simple language like 'fire her!'"

"You can't tell me who to fire in my own house," Bob informed her.

"It used to be my house, too, and Mikey's," Connie returned proudly. "Now it seems to be Teresa's."

Bob seemed to realize all at once what was happening to his life. "She's just the housekeeper," he began.

"That's right," Connie replied. "But you don't treat her like one."

"You don't treat me like a husband," he retorted.

Connie didn't answer him. "Say good-night to everyone, Mikey," she told their son.

"Good night," he said obligingly.

Connie smiled apologetically at Lang and Kirry, ignored the others and stalked out the door with Mikey. Minutes later, her car started up and moved out of the driveway around Lang's.

Bob's eyes narrowed. "Connie isn't my wife, she's the resident mechanic. She has no time for anything except her damned job! Mikey and I were just flotsam, don't you realize that? She doesn't want to be a wife and mother, she wants a career! Okay, I let her have it. But it's not working out."

Kirry stared at Bob with carefully concealed horror. Was she seeing what marriage to Lang would be like, except in reverse? Would he only have time for his job, and his family would be little more than an afterthought?

Lang, too, was having some difficulties with his thoughts. Kirry loved her job, too. She would be like Connie, trying to juggle a job and children, if she had any. It would be a division of loyalties that could be managed, if she loved and was loved enough. But he was seeing in Bob's relationship with Connie all the inherent dangers of marriage. He didn't like what he saw. He'd had cold feet before about marriage. They were ice-cold now.

"See what you're asking for?" Bob asked Lang with a humorless laugh. "She said she wanted a husband and a family, but what she really wanted was a garage. You'd better agree beforehand about what kind of marriage you're going to have," he said bitterly.

"Did you ever tell Connie how you felt?" Kirry asked hesitantly.

"Until I was blue in the face, but it's always been what Connie wants, not what I want." He glanced at Teresa as she came into the room, shy and quiet. "Are you leaving, too?"

Teresa explained in Spanish that she wanted to go to her brother's home in San Antonio. She asked if Lang and Kirry would drop her off.

"Come on, Teresa," Lang said. "You can ride with us."

"Muchas gracias." She walked to Bob and looked up at him with those huge, soft eyes. *"Lo siento. No te puse furioso a mi, por favor,"* she whispered.

Bob's face contorted. "Of course I'm not mad at you," he said softly, and his expression and tone got through even if the words didn't quite register.

She smiled at him. *"Hasta luego. ¿Nos vamos?"*

Lang nodded. "We go. I'll be in touch, Bob."

Bob hesitated. "Don't...blame me too much," he said miserably.

Lang moved forward and hugged him warmly. "You're my brother, you idiot, I only want you to be happy."

Nine

Lang and Kirry dropped Teresa off at her brother's house on the outskirts of San Antonio. Lang went with her to the door, explaining that his sister-in-law had left the house for the night—without going into any detail about the reason for it—and that it wouldn't be fitting for Teresa to spend the night alone with Bob. The brother was gracious and appreciative, and Lang came back to the car feeling less sad.

"She's got a nice family," he told Kirry.

"Your brother is really smitten with her," Kirry replied. "I'm sorry for Connie, because I don't think Bob is going to be able to resist Teresa."

"Don't be so sure," he said curtly.

"You're worried."

"I believe in marriage. Sometimes people give up too easily on a relationship."

"Sometimes they hang on to one that has no future."

He glanced at her, and his eyes became searching on her face. "Connie shouldn't have married," he said. "She should have opened her own garage and spent years building it up before she settled down."

"Yes."

He sighed heavily. "You don't really want to get married yet, do you?" he asked with his attention on the road ahead. "You want a career, just like Connie."

Her heart leaped. Was that what he thought, that a job meant more to her than making a home for Lang and their children? Or was that what he wanted to think? Was he looking for a way to break the engagement already? It felt like a replay of the past.

She twisted her fingers in her lap and watched them tangle and untangle. "Some women aren't cut out to be mothers, I think," she said. "Connie loves Mikey, but she's never been particularly maternal."

"It's a little late for her to find it out," he said angrily.

"Perhaps she didn't know herself," she said.

He didn't reply. He was taking it hard. Unusually hard.

She glanced at him. "Some men aren't cut out to be fathers, either, I guess."

He stiffened. "Really?"

"You freeze up every time someone mentions a family, Lang, haven't you realized?"

His hands gripped the steering wheel and then relaxed. "Children mean permanent ties."

"I know." She smiled. "You aren't ready, anymore than Connie was."

"Neither are you," he returned angrily. "You want a career."

"Of course I do. Everyone wants to make their mark in the world, but it's possible to combine a career with a family," she said, laughing. "People do it all the time."

"Like Connie has?" he asked angrily.

"Connie is having trouble. She's acting too single-mindedly to juggle a job and a family."

"Juggle them!" he snapped.

Kirry was surprised at the antagonism in his deep voice. She knew that the Patton boys had lost their mother when they were just a little older than Mikey, but Lang never spoke of her. Their father had raised them and he'd died when Kirry and Lang were just noticing each other.

"Lang, you never talk about your mother," she remarked.

"I never will."

She was shocked at the vehemence in the assertion. "Not even to me?"

"What do you want to know about her?" he asked. She hesitated. "What was she like?"

"She was a career woman," he said with a cold smile, glancing her way. "She was one of those women who should never have married. She didn't have time for Bob and me. She was too busy flying all over the country to sell real estate. And one day she went up in a plane that was due for an overhaul, but she couldn't wait because she might miss a sale. The plane went down and we buried her in pieces."

Her breath caught in her throat. "Oh, Lang, I'm so sorry."

"Why? We never loved her, damn her," he retorted. "She never loved us, either. We were a nuisance, an inconvenience. She told our father every time they had a fight that she never wanted us in the first place, but he'd worried her to death about wanting kids, so she gave in. We were her greatest regret. She didn't remember a birthday the whole time we were kids, and she never remembered Christmas presents. I made her an ashtray at school in clay and painted it her favorite colors. She threw it in the trash."

Why hadn't he ever told her this? She realized then that Lang had never shared his deepest feelings with her. In all the years she'd known him, he'd never spoken of his childhood at all—until now. And she understood for the first time why he was so reluctant to marry.

"You think it will be the same for us," she said suddenly. "You think I'll be like your mother."

He looked in the rearview mirror before he made the next turn, with smooth ease. "Won't you, Kirry?" he asked with world-weary cynicism. "This is the era of single-parent families. I know all about that. I was the product of one, even if my parents were married on paper. I was a latchkey kid from the age of six. Would you like to hear some horror stories that came from it?"

"I can imagine," she said. Her soft eyes slid over his face. "It's a different world. Life-styles are changing almost overnight. What used to be the norm isn't anymore. We can't go back to the past, Lang. We all have to adjust. With the economy in its present state, most families can't make it on one income, so women have to work. If we did get married, I'd still have to have a job."

He grimaced. He didn't like what she was saying. It was all too true. They could hardly have a decent standard of living and children on just his salary, as good as it was. And what if he became disabled? If Kirry couldn't work, how would she support herself and their family if something happened to him?

"It's not such a bad thing, a woman being independent," she said gently.

"My mother certainly was," he said.

He turned into the parking lot of the building where they lived, closemouthed and quiet. Old memories were hurting him. He didn't like remembering his mother and her single-minded devotion to the almighty job. His father worked as a laborer at a feed mill. He didn't make a lot of money and he worked long hours, so he wasn't home when Bob and Lang got home from school.

Their mother could have had time for them if she'd wanted to. She was pretty much self-employed. Her job schedule could have been rearranged. But she was always gone. And when she was home, she expected Lang and Bob to have the housework done and wait on her because she was tired.

Their father had done his best to accommodate her, and that had made Lang and Bob resentful and angry at the way she used him. When she died in the plane crash, their standard of living dropped radically. But Lang hadn't cried. Neither had Bob. Their father had tried to explain it once, to make them understand that she'd loved them, in her way, but she hadn't wanted to get married in the first place. He'd compromised her, and they'd had to, for her parents' sake. In those days, in a small Texas town, church-going girls didn't have babies out of wedlock.

"My parents had to get married," Lang muttered, staring into the past.

"I'm sorry."

He cut off the engine and turned to her. "Why were you having chills?" he demanded. "Could Connie have been right with that shot in the dark?"

"We used something," she said weakly.

"And nothing is foolproof." He looked haunted. "Tell me!"

"I can't tell you what I don't know, Lang," she replied very quietly. "It's way too soon to even guess yet."

He relented. His hand ruffled his own hair as he leaned back in the seat. "I don't want you to be pregnant, Kirry," he said.

She felt her body stiffen. That was blunt enough. "You can't forgive your mother, so I'm to be punished for her sins, is that it?"

He looked puzzled. "That has nothing to do with it."

"Sure." She opened the car door and got out. Her legs felt shaky. Her self-confidence was on the blink entirely.

He got out, too, and followed her into the building and the elevator. He rammed his hands into his pockets and stared at her broodingly as they went up.

"Don't pretend that you'd be thrilled about it any more than I would," he persisted.

She didn't look at him or answer him.

They got off on their floor and she paused at the door of her apartment. "Lorna said that you didn't want to live here anymore. You denied it, but was it true?"

He frowned as he studied her. Lorna's threat came back full force. She was a vindictive woman, and Lang knew from the past that she didn't bluff.

"What if you lost your job, Kirry?"

"I'd find another," she said. "I'm not hopelessly untalented."

"If you left under a cloud, it might be difficult to find something else as good."

"I'm not going to be fired," she said heavily. "Lorna may not like me, but Mack does, and he can clear me with the Lancasters. It isn't as if I've done something unforgivable."

He looked worried and couldn't hide it. His dark eyes searched her green ones quietly. She didn't know what Lorna had threatened. He couldn't tell her, either.

"Are you sure that there won't be any consequences from what we did?" he asked heavily.

"You're worrying it to death because of one idle remark Connie made! Lang, I'm not pregnant, all right?"

"All right." He laughed at his own concern. He was overreacting. "Then if you're that sure, maybe it would be better if we let the engagement fade away."

Her eyes narrowed. "That's what Lorna wants, I gather?"

He hesitated. "Yes," he said. "That's what she wants." He didn't add why.

She searched his face as if she were saying goodbye. In fact, she was. "Then give her what she wants," she replied. "I don't want to sacrifice my future to your conscience. The only reason you wanted the engagement in the first place was because you felt guilty that we slept together. That's a bad reason to marry someone, especially when there is no possibility of any consequences," she added firmly.

Women were supposed to know if they were pregnant, he assured himself. She sounded confident. Right now, getting Lorna out of the picture before she could damage Kirry's future was the most important thing. Let her think she'd won. Yes.

"Consider the engagement off, then, if that's what you want," he said.

She managed a smile, but it was strained. "It's what you want," she said, pointedly. "You can't let go of the past, can you? I never knew why you really wanted out. You never told me anything about your life, and I didn't even realize it. You wanted me. That's all it ever was."

He didn't deny it, but his face was taut and his eyes unreadable.

She turned away. "That's what I thought," she said quietly, as she unlocked her door.

Lang watched her hungrily, averting his eyes when she looked back at him.

"I'll still be around," he reminded her. "Don't let your guard down where Erikson's concerned. And if you'd rather not keep the lessons going with me, I'll have one of my advanced students work with you. It would be a shame to stop now."

"Whatever you think," she agreed complacently.

His eyes were weary. "Maybe I am living in the past," he said then. "The fact is, I don't want children and I can't settle for half a marriage. I'm sorry. Sex isn't enough."

She knew her face had gone pale, but she smiled like a trooper. "No, it isn't," she agreed. "See you around, Lang."

He nodded. He couldn't trust himself to speak.

She closed the door with a firm click and Lang stood staring at it with his heart in his eyes for a long moment before he turned and went back to his own apartment. It had never seemed as empty in the past.

Kirry lay awake most of the night, thinking about Lang's comments. Somehow she couldn't equate the man who'd said sex wasn't enough with the incredibly tender lover of the other night. It had been much, much more than physical lust. But he wouldn't acknowledge it. And he'd seemed withdrawn the night before, especially when she'd mentioned Lorna. She didn't know what was going on, but it had to have something to do with her job. Was she going to be fired? Did he know something she didn't?

Perhaps he'd made that suggestion about an alternate campaign for a purpose. When she got up the next day, it was with a new resolve. She wasn't going to hang around and wait to be bumped from the company roster. She had some good ideas. Lorna might not appreciate them, but she knew someone who would. She put in her notice that very morning, cautioning Mack not to share it with the Lancasters just yet. He agreed, feeling personally that Kirry had been deliberately dealt a bad hand through Lorna's catty remarks to her friend, Mrs. Lancaster.

Kirry went to see Reflections, Inc., on her lunch hour. It was a new public relations firm, and the owner had a lean and hungry look. He hired Kirry on the spot when he heard some of her ideas, even going so far as to offer her a percentage of the business as well as a salary if she pulled in new business for them. Her feet hardly left the pavement on the way back to work. Marrying Lang would have made her float twice as high, but now the job would have to be her satisfaction. If she allowed herself to think about losing Lang again, she'd go mad.

By the time she got ready to leave the office, much later than she'd planned to, she'd forgotten all about Erikson in the joy of the day. Her mind was on her new position and the delight she was going to feel when she walked out the door for the last time. Her only regret was poor Mack. His ideas weren't pleasing Lorna, and she was taking out most of her frustrations on him. Everyone in the office could hear her displeasure.

"I'll cope," he'd told Kirry, tongue in cheek. "When she's had enough, she'll go looking for another agency. The joke will be on the Lancasters, not me."

Kirry had to agree, and she couldn't help feeling a little sting of pleasure at the thought. Mrs. Lancaster hadn't learned that friendship had to be kept separate from business if she wanted her company to prosper. By allowing Lorna to manipulate her, she'd cost herself a lot of new business. And an employee who could have helped her keep it.

She was thinking about the markets she could help bring to Reflections, Inc., when she suddenly realized that it was dark and she was alone in the parking lot.

Her car was in plain view, and the lot was lighted. She looked around quickly, but there wasn't another car in sight. She was being paranoid, she told herself. Erikson hadn't been seen all day. It was highly unlikely that he'd be laying in wait for her tonight.

She had her keys in her hand, locked in between her fingers to make a formidable weapon if necessary. She walked quickly and her eyes darted around cautiously. She unlocked the car, but before she got in, she looked in the back seat. Then she dashed inside and locked the doors again. Safe!

There was nothing suspicious in the interior, and she checked carefully. Then she started the car and put it in gear. No Erickson. She'd worried for nothing.

She turned the car out into traffic and drove toward her apartment building. It had been a very profitable day. She wondered how Lang had fared, and if Bob and Connie had talked over their differences. It would be sad for little Mikey if his parents divorced. She felt sorry for all of them. She felt sorriest for Lang and herself.

As she pulled into the parking lot of her apartment building and turned off the engine, she looked around cautiously. But there were other people nearby and she relaxed. Nothing to worry about, she assured herself. He was going to give it up. She knew he was. She felt better about everything.

She got her purse and locked the car, pulling her coat closer against the chilly night air. Her eyes sparkled as she thought about her one pleasure, the change of jobs.

She walked into the apartment building and got into the elevator with a couple of other tenants. Nobody spoke. She got off on her floor, wondering as she walked down the hall if Lang was at home. She stared at his door, but she only hesitated for an instant. He'd made his feelings clear. She was no longer part of his life. In fact, he might have even moved out by now. She was just going to have to learn how to live without him.

She unlocked her apartment door, idly aware that it was unusually easy to get into tonight, and closed and locked it behind her. She turned on the light and walked into her bedroom to change clothes.

As she entered the room, an arm came around her neck and trapped her, hurting.

"Hello, girlie." A familiar voice chuckled. "Did you think I'd forget about you? Not a chance! It's payback time, blondie."

Her heart ran wild. Her knees felt like jelly. He was hurting her and in a minute he'd cut off her wind. She had to keep her head. If she panicked, it was all over.

"Mr. Erikson, you'll go to jail." She got the warning out through dry lips.

"Do you think so? It will be my word against yours. Nobody will believe you." His free hand touched her blatantly over her jacket. "Nice. You feel real nice...."

Now or never, she thought. Now or never. Her heartbeat went wild as she came back with her elbow right into his diaphragm as hard as she could. His intake of breath and the relaxing of the arm around her neck told its own story.

She whirled, acting instinctively, all Lang's training firmly in place as she brought up her knee into his groin and then stepped in, broke his balance and sent him careening down onto the floor.

Get out, she heard a voice in her head, *don't be a heroine.* She ran for the front door. Her hands fumbled with the lock, but only for a second. She got the door open and ran into the hall. Her hands beat on Lang's door, and she screamed, but he wasn't home. The hall was deserted! She heard noises coming from her apartment.

She ran to the elevator, giving way to panic, and pressed the button repeatedly. But the elevator didn't budge. She remembered the warning about the stairwell, but she was too frightened to heed it. It was the only way out.

She ran into the stairwell and tripped going down the steps, straining the muscles in her ankle so that each new step was painful. She was breathing raggedly now, and every breath hurt. A sob caught in her throat as she made it to the ground level and burst out into the lobby.

The security guard frowned as he saw her, and he came toward her at once, with a hand on the gun at his hip.

"Are you all right, Miss Campbell?" he asked quickly. "What's happened?"

"In my...apartment. A man. He attacked me," she gasped.

His face went taut. He took her to the manager's office and handed her over to a concerned clerk, who took her in back while the security guard went into the stairwell.

Kirry knew what he was going to find. Erikson was too savvy to let himself be caught. He'd be long gone, and out for blood now. She'd hurt his pride. It wouldn't be a game to him anymore. He'd want to kill her.

Nausea rose in her throat, making her sick all over. The clerk helped her to the rest room, just in time. She was white and drawn when she went back to the office, to find that the security guard was back, and grim-faced.

"I knew he'd be gone," she whispered unsteadily. "But I hurt him."

"He got out over the balcony. Somebody must have seen him, though," he told her. "Nobody gets away with that sort of thing in my building," he added coldly. "Is there someone you can stay with, Miss Campbell, for tonight? I don't like thinking about you being up there alone."

She laughed bitterly. It hadn't occurred to her before that she had nothing in her life except friendly acquaintances like Betty. She had no family in this country; God only knew where her mother was, and there wasn't anyone else.

"No," she said, choking down tears. "I have no one."

He looked worried. He scowled as he tried to come up with a solution. "We'll have to call the police," he said.

She didn't have the strength to argue. Her will-power was at its lowest ebb in years.

The police came and questioned her. She gave them a description of Erikson, explaining the problem and referring them to people at her office—and to Lang.

"We'll pick him up," a young officer said coldly. "He can't be too hard to find."

"Good thing you knew some self-defense, young lady," his older partner added. "I taught my daughter when she was just a kid. It's handy stuff."

"You can say that again," she agreed with a wan smile.

"I've called in one of our part-time security guards," the apartment security officer said, rejoining them with a taut expression. "He'll be outside your apartment all night long, Miss Campbell. You needn't worry."

She felt tears sliding down her cheeks. "Oh, it's so kind . . . !" she whispered.

He looked embarrassed. "You're a tenant," he said. "We can't have people upsetting our tenants. Here, now, don't do that. It's all over."

The cluster of people in the lobby piqued Lang's curiosity as he came into the apartment building. He'd had to interview applicants and then there had been a faulty burglar alarm that had to be dealt with. He was worn from the rigors of the day, and from hating what he'd done to Kirry. Damn Lorna, he wasn't going to let her dictate his life or intimidate Kirry. He'd told her so, too. And, he'd added, if she told the Lancasters about Kirry, he'd have something to tell them about her.

She hadn't expected that. Her face had gone pale and she'd blustered around for ten minutes. But in the end, she'd given in. She had other men in her life, she'd informed him. She didn't need to drag up old relationships to keep her warm, and she didn't want him, anyway.

Lang had felt sorry for her. But not sorry enough to hang around. He was guilty over the way he'd treated Kirry, and he'd done some hard thinking about his position on marriage. He was overreacting because of his mother, Kirry had said, and she was right. He'd come back with the intention of telling her so, and suggesting that they might think about starting over one more time. But there would be no more secrets. And whatever problems they encountered, they'd work out.

But the commotion near the manager's office distracted him. He walked toward it, and suddenly saw Kirry's white face and torn blouse. Erikson!

He pushed his way through the crush of police officers to her, and without a word, he pulled her into his arms and wrapped her up there.

"Are you all right?" he asked without a greeting.

She was stiff in his arms, but she didn't push him away. "Erikson was waiting for me in the apartment.

I remembered just enough of what you taught me to get away in time. But he's vanished. They're searching for him now."

Lang lifted his head and looked into her eyes. She was putting up a good front, but that was fear in her face.

"Damn him," he said through his teeth.

"We're posting a man outside her apartment," the security guard began.

"To hell with that. I'm taking her to my brother and sister-in-law's home. She'll be safe," he said abruptly.

"That would be the best thing you could do," one of the policemen said. "We'll get him. But she'll be safer where he can't find her."

"I'll take care of her." Lang turned to the security guard. "Thanks," he said huskily.

The other man shrugged and smiled. So that was the way of things. Nice young woman, and that beau of hers was pretty protective. She'd be looked after.

Ten

Lang waited for her to change and pack in her apartment, while he telephoned Bob and explained what had happened.

"Come on down," Bob said in a subdued tone. "Connie and Mikey came back today."

"And Teresa?" Lang asked.

"I was a fool. Connie isn't speaking to me, but if you bring Kirry, maybe it will help all of us out."

"I'll see you shortly. And thanks."

He hung up. Kirry was still standing in the doorway of her bedroom, in the same clothes.

"You haven't changed," he said gently.

"I don't want to go in there alone," she said with a self-conscious laugh. "Silly, isn't it?"

"Not at all. I think you're pretty brave," he said, smiling.

She smiled back. "I don't feel it. I was sick."

"No wonder." He came into the bedroom with her. "What do you want to wear?"

She laid out some jeans and a top. Before she could move, he did, to begin undressing her.

She looked up at him like a child, her eyes wide, curious.

He smiled at her tenderly. "I could learn to like this," he remarked as he stripped her out of everything except her briefs and bra. "You're exquisitely designed, Miss Campbell."

"I feel weak all over."

"Do you?" He pulled her close and bent to kiss her with breathless tenderness. His hands slid down to her hips and his thumbs spread over her belly. He lifted his head and searched her eyes while he touched her gently. "So do I. My knees buckle when I kiss you."

That made her laugh. "They do not."

He rubbed his nose against hers. "How do you know? You aren't looking down."

She drew in a slow breath and her face was worried. "Did I hear you say that Connie was back with Bob?"

"For the time being. He's come to his senses."

"Maybe she has, too." She lifted her hand to his face and had to fight tears at the hunger she felt for his love. "I wish..."

"What?" he asked softly.

She withdrew her hand. "Nothing. We should go."

"With you like that?" he asked. "We'd be arrested."

"If you'll let me go, I'll get dressed."

"No, I don't like that idea," he murmured. "Covering up such a beautiful body ought to qualify as a crime."

She blushed and laughed. "Lang!"

He tilted her face up and kissed her with slow, sweet ardor. "We could make love before we go," he whispered. His hands moved up to her breasts and teased them, possessed them. "Would you like to?"

"We've already agreed that it isn't a good idea if we see each other," she protested weakly.

"That was before," he murmured against her lips.

"Before what?"

"Before I discovered that I wouldn't mind if we had a baby together."

Her body stilled against him. She lifted her eyes to his and found warm, dark secrets in them. "Wh...what?"

He bent and lifted her into his arms. "You'll still have to work," he said as he carried her to the bed. "I make good money, but we'll have a better life-style with two salaries. Besides that, you need to be self-supporting. We can find a good day-care center, one that we both feel comfortable with, and I'll learn to do diapers and feed him...unless you want to?" he added with a wickedly sensuous smile as his eyes dropped to her breasts.

She shivered with the force of her feelings. "Oh, yes, I'd like...to," she moaned. "Lang, I love you so much," she sobbed. "More than my life...!"

He eased over her and pressed her gently down into the mattress. His mouth covered hers and his hands found fastenings and revealed the soft bareness of her body to his mouth and his hands and his eyes.

"I love you," he whispered back. "It was the thought of a family that unsettled me. I didn't even know why, until you made me realize how badly my childhood had scarred me. But I think I can come to terms with it. The one thing I can't do is walk away from you twice in one lifetime. So we'll just have to cope."

"We will. I know we will." Her heart was in her eyes as she looked up at him. "Lang?"

"Hmm?" he murmured against her throat.

"Could you take your clothes off?"

He chuckled. "I guess so. Want to watch?"

Her breath caught. "Yes," she whispered, her eyes wide and ardent.

He laughed unsteadily as he stood and pulled off everything that concealed his powerful body from her. When he turned back to the bed, she shivered a little in anticipation, because she knew now what pleasure he could give her.

He slid down beside her, his eyes warm and alive with the joy of what they were sharing. "We can use something, if you want to."

She pulled him down with loving arms. "You're so certain that I can't be a wife and a mother at the same time, aren't you?" she asked gently. "Why don't you let me show you?"

"Darlin'," he whispered as he covered her open mouth with his, "I'd love nothing better!"

She opened her arms to him as his body moved down to press against hers. For endless minutes, they lost themselves in the soft caresses that led to the urgent, slow, sweet rhythm of love. There was a new tenderness in the expression of it, but the passion was just as familiar as the upswing of frenetic pleasure that left them shuddering in its exquisite aftermath.

"My God," he groaned into her mouth as his full weight descended on her. "Am I dreaming?"

"I hope not," she whispered, shaken. Her legs tangled in his and she pressed her face into his damp throat. "The world trembled, didn't it?"

He laughed. "And a few other things," he murmured dryly.

"I love the way you love me," she whispered. "I love you."

"Show me again," he said against her mouth, and his hips shifted slowly against hers. "Make me cry out."

"But can you?" she asked uncertainly.

He moved sharply and chuckled at her wide-eyed wonder. "Let's see," he murmured, and pushed down.

It was three hours later when they arrived at Bob and Connie's house.

"We were getting worried," Bob said as they climbed out of the car in his driveway. "Kirry, are you all right?"

"Oh, I'm fine," she assured him with a smile. "I'm a little sore, but that's normal."

"She laid Erikson out," Lang added with pride, glad that his brother couldn't see the flush on his high cheekbones. "I appreciate your letting us come down."

"What are family for? Connie, they're here!"

Connie came out, in a dress, looking subdued and so feminine that Lang actually leaned forward for a closer look. "Connie?" he asked, shocked.

She glared at him. "Yes, it's me, can't you recognize me when I'm not covered in grease?" she asked caustically.

He grinned. "Well, come to think of it, no," he teased.

She had her arms tight over her breasts and she wasn't looking at Bob. She moved them to hug Kirry. "Are you all right, honey?" she asked, concerned.

"I'm fine," Kirry said, smiling helplessly at Lang. "We're engaged," she told them.

"You've already told us, don't you remember?" Connie asked gently.

They hadn't known about the engagement being broken. Kirry and Lang exchanged glances and smiles.

"No use expecting any sense out of you two." Bob chuckled. "Come on in. Mikey's gone to bed. We'll have some coffee and cake."

"My cake, not hers," Connie said sharply to Bob, who looked uncomfortable. "I just baked it. I can cook."

"Honey, I never said you couldn't," Bob began.

"Hmmph!" she muttered, and led the way into the house.

"She's been like that since she got here," Bob said miserably. "She treats me like an adulterer. I swear to God, I never put a hand on Teresa."

"Have you told Connie that?"

"Would she listen?" he muttered.

"If you tell her the right way, she might," Lang mused, his eyes warm and loving on Kirry as she went into the kitchen with Connie.

Bob glanced at his brother curiously. "Are you serious this time about marrying Kirry?" he asked.

Lang paused, sticking his hands into his pockets. "I'm serious," he said. "I guess the way we grew up had a worse effect on me than it did on you, Bob," he added. "I couldn't bear the thought of bringing a child into the world whose mother treated it like a nuisance."

"I can't believe you thought Kirry would be like our mother," he mused. "Kirry's a motherly type."

"Not anymore," Lang told him, with a sense of pride. "She's got a good mind and she should use it. Besides that, she's one of the best karate students I've ever trained," he added with a chuckle. "Erikson attacked her and she laid him out." His eyes sparkled with quick temper. "Damn him, I hope we can put him away forever. If she hadn't known what to do, the least that would have happened is that she'd have been raped. He might even have killed her."

Bob frowned. "What did she do to him?"

"He was a security guard at the office. She objected to being talked to like a prostitute."

Bob's eyebrows rose. "How did he keep his job so long, with that sort of attitude?"

"Women have kept quiet about harassment in the past. They've started objecting to it, and so they should. You know, in the early days of the century, despite the fact that women weren't permitted the freedom men enjoyed, at least they were treated with respect. A man who insulted a woman, married or single, could expect to be beaten within an inch of his life. These days, you'd be surprised at the language men feel comfortable using around them."

"Listen, have you ever heard Connie when she hit her thumb with a hammer?" Bob mused.

Lang clapped his brother on the back. "Point taken."

Kirry's bad experience was the talk of the evening, but the looks she and Lang were exchanging amused Bob.

"I guess you still haven't set a date," he commented.

"Next week," Lang said easily, smiling at Kirry's surprise. "If you don't want a big wedding, that is."

"I just want you," Kirry said honestly. "A justice of the peace and a simple wedding ring will suit me fine."

"That's how Connie and I did it," Bob said, his dark eyes searching his wife's subdued face. "We used to sit up all hours just talking. We were good friends long before we wanted to live together. And when Mikey came along, he was the beginning of the whole world."

Connie's eyes softened as she remembered her son's birth. She stared at Bob with pain in her whole expression. "And you're willing to throw away ten good years for a little girl playing house."

His face hardened. "At least she likes it."

"For now," Connie agreed. "But she's very young. When she gets a few more years on her, she'll realize that a woman has to be a person in her own right, not just an extension of her husband. Thinking up new recipes isn't enough anymore."

"Keeping a clean house and raising good children who were loved and given attention used to be enough," Bob said angrily.

"Of course it did," his wife replied with a sad smile. "But the world has changed. It's so tough on one salary. When I worked, I could afford so many nice things that we could never have before. I guess I went wild." She shrugged, glancing uncertainly at Bob. "I almost lost my family in the process. I've decided that I want to be a mechanic, but that I don't want it more than I want you and Mikey."

Bob studied the coffee cup in front of him. "I don't want to start getting used to another person this late in my life," he confessed.

She smiled. "I could work for someone . . ."

He looked up. "You could work at your own shop, in the back," he said stiffly. "But you can close up on Wednesdays and Saturdays, and we'll spend those days, and Sunday, as a family. Meanwhile, having someone to help keep the house clean isn't a bad idea." Before she could speak, he added, "I know a teenage boy who likes to cook and doesn't mind cleaning. Mrs. Jones's son, and he could use the money because he wants to go to one of those French cooking schools when he gets out of school."

Connie was surprised. "But you hate my work!"

"I was jealous of it," he confessed with a smile. He looked at his brother. "I guess Lang and I never talked enough about how we were raised. We were a dysfunctional family and never even knew it. Now we're both having to learn that marriage is what you make of it."

Connie's face had brightened. She flushed when Bob smiled warmly at her, and he chuckled. "It isn't so bad, having a mechanic in the family. Except that my car sure does run rough," he added.

"I can fix it," Connie mused.

"I know."

Kirry felt Lang's hand curving around hers where it lay on the table. She looked at him with her heart in her eyes, and his breath caught.

"Where are you going to live when you're married?" Bob asked them, breaking the spell.

"I like the security where we are," Lang said with a chuckle. "My apartment or hers, it doesn't matter. I'd live with her in a mud hut," he added solemnly.

"That goes double for me," she said softly.

"Until the kids come along," he added very slowly, holding her eyes. "Then I think we might want a house. One with a big yard, so we can have a dog."

There were tears of pure joy in her eyes.

"Will you go on working for Lancaster, Inc.?" Connie asked her.

Kirry caught her breath. "Oh, that reminds me!" And she told them what she'd done, and about her new job.

Lang burst out laughing. "And I thought you weren't listening when I suggested it."

"I was listening. Mack says Mrs. Lancaster is going to be very sorry indeed, because Lorna is already talking about pulling the account."

"That doesn't surprise me in the least," Lang ventured. "I'm sorry that Lorna gave you a hard time. I hope you believe that I was serious when I said there was nothing between us."

"Oh, of course I do," she assured him. It would be impossible to believe anything else, when he looked at her that way, with everything he felt naked in his face.

"What will they do to that man when they catch him?" Connie asked, concerned. "Will there be enough evidence to keep him locked up?"

Lang was remembering the times Erikson had gotten away with what he'd done, and he was worried. "I hope so."

Kirry was thinking the same thing. She clung to Lang's hand and tried not to brood about it. She had visions of a long, drawn-out court case and legal expenses that would bankrupt them.

"Don't worry about it," Lang said softly. He bent and kissed her forehead softly. "We'll work it all out. I promise you we will."

They stayed the night, parting reluctantly as she went to the guest room and Lang bedded down on the sofa. She didn't want to be away from him long enough to sleep. Apparently he felt the same way, because in the early hours of the morning, he picked her up out of the bed and carried her back to the sofa, bundling her up in his arms until morning.

Connie and Bob came upon them like that, and stood looking down at them with indulgent smiles, their arms around each other.

"Remember how that felt?" Bob asked gently. "To be so much in love that you can't bear the agony of being apart even for a few hours?"

"Oh, yes." Connie reached up and kissed him. "I still feel like that. It's why I came home."

He smiled and drew her close. "So do I. I'm glad we both woke up in time, Connie."

"Marriage has to have compromise or it can't last. For Mikey's sake, and our own, I'm glad we're both reasonable people."

He chuckled. "After last night, I'm not sure that I'm very reasonable anymore. In fact, I think I'm loopy." He whispered in her ear, "Did you really do that, or did I dream it?"

She flushed scarlet. "Bob!"

The cry woke Lang and Kirry. They blinked and stared up at their hosts. Lang smiled sheepishly. "This isn't quite what it looks like..."

"Looks like two people in love to me." Bob chuckled. "Come and have breakfast, you idiots."

Later in the day, Lang and Kirry drove back up to San Antonio. Both of them were anxious to see if any progress had been made about Erikson. What they discovered shocked them.

"It was kind of tragic, in a way," the police lieutenant who spoke to them at the precinct said matter-of-factly. "He was going too fast and just shot right off the bridge, through the railing. We found him a few hours ago. I tried to call you both, but no one was at home."

"We were at my brother's house in Floresville," Lang said. He pulled Kirry closer. "It's been a hell of a few weeks."

"Yes, I know. This isn't the only stalking case we've ever had," the policeman replied. "I've talked to one of our legislators, and he's willing to introduce some legislation about it. He'd like to talk to you, Miss Campbell."

"I'd like to talk to him," she replied quietly.

"At any rate, you're safe now," he told her. "Try not to let it scar you. The world is full of people who enjoy hurting other people. It's why I have a job."

"Thanks."

They walked out into the sunlight, and Kirry clung to Lang's hand.

"This is why women put up with it," she said uneasily.

"What?"

"Harassment on the job," she said simply. "They're afraid of something like what happened to me. They're afraid of being the object of gossip by other employees, or being fired, or being discriminated against. Even if you keep your job, people still resent you. Even some women think it's stupid for a woman to cause trouble because a man is vulgar in front of her, or because he makes sexist remarks."

He turned to her. "Nobody ever promised that life was easy. Sometimes it's dangerous to do the right thing. Sometimes it causes heartache. That doesn't change the fact that people have a right to work unmolested."

She hesitated. Then she nodded. "All the same, I don't know if I'd have enough courage to do it again after what happened to me."

He chuckled. "Really? I think you have enough courage."

"You're prejudiced."

"I love you to distraction," he said simply. "Doesn't it show?"

Her eyes sparkled with delight as she looked at him. "Cold turkey and in broad daylight, even! You must mean it."

"Didn't you believe me?"

"Yes," she said after a minute. "I didn't really think I could care so much about you unless you cared about me, too."

"Smart lady. When do you leave Lancaster, Inc.?"

"Monday after next. I got a raise, too, at Reflections, Inc."

He grinned. "Even better. Will it involve as much traveling as you're doing now?"

"No," she replied, her face bright. "Because I told my new boss that I wanted to be home at nights, and he said that he's got two single employees who love to travel, and they'll carry the ball in that respect. I may have to go out of town occasionally, but it won't be every week."

"That I can handle." He pursed his lips. "My job will keep me in town, thank God, so if you have to be away, I can mind the kids."

"Kids? Plural?"

His eyes slid over her with kindling desire and slow pleasure. "I thought a boy and a girl would be nice."

"Did you, now? Boys run in your family for three generations and I'm the first girl in my family in two. The odds are against little girls." He started to speak and she put her fingers over his mouth, smiling. "I like playing baseball, don't you remember? And I never did play with dolls."

He chuckled. "Okay. We'll see what we get."

"Why don't we go home, since we don't have to go in to the office today, and you can see what you get."

He whistled softly. "My knees are going weak."

"So are mine." She pressed close to him as they walked toward the car. She allowed herself a little pity for Erikson. "He didn't have a family, did he?" she asked.

He knew who she meant. "No."

"Poor man. He was sick, Lang. Sick in the mind. I'm sorry for him."

"So am I, in a way. But it was fate, honey. I'm glad you're safe. I'll take care of you."

She liked that protectiveness in him. She nuzzled her face against his shoulder. "I'll take care of you, too, my darling."

He kissed her forehead. "Let's stop by city hall and get the marriage license. Then," he added softly, "we'll see how wicked we can get behind closed doors."

She didn't have an argument with that.

They were married less than a week later, with Bob and Connie and Mikey for witnesses, and they managed a brief honeymoon trip to Jamaica. When they came back, Kirry started her new job and found it much to her liking. The Lancasters lost the Lorna McLane account in short order, along with the promise of new customers. They apologized to Kirry, once they found out just how Lorna had twisted things to make her look incompetent. Kirry accepted the apology gracefully, but wouldn't return, even though Lang stayed with them. There were no hard feelings, and the Lancasters gave them a handsome belated wedding present of a silver service.

"That was nice of them," Kirry remarked later as she was lying in Lang's big arms in bed.

"I thought so, too." He opened one eye as she propped over him. "You lost your breakfast this morning. Was it something that didn't sit well on your stomach?"

She smiled wickedly. "It's something that probably will sit well on my stomach until it gets too big."

Both eyes opened, with love and soft wonder. "Are we sure yet?" he asked with a glowing smile.

She nodded. "I got one of those kits this morning, and did it twice. I'll go to the doctor to make sure, but there won't be any surprises."

He pulled her down and kissed her tenderly, smiling against her mouth. "Are you sure we're going to have a boy?"

She laughed. "There's absolutely no chance that it will be anything else," she said smugly, and squealed when his fingers dug gently into her ribs.

Seven months later, Lang stood in the hospital room with Cecily Maureen Patton in his arms and one eyebrow lifted with superior irony down at his pretty wife.

"Go ahead," she challenged. "I know you're dying to say it."

He chuckled. Then his face sobered and he looked at Kirry with such love that she flushed. "Thank you," he said gently. "I never knew what life was all about until they put her in my arms."

"I know," she replied with wonder. "Lang, I've never felt like this. To know that we did that, that we created something so incredible between us."

"And had such delight from doing it," he teased gently, loving her soft flush. He looked down at his daughter. "Isn't she a beauty? Daddy loves little girls," he cooed as he kissed the tiny face. "He'll take her on picnics and buy her toys and kill boys who break her heart. Daddy will teach her to shoot guns, and do martial arts, and track spies..."

"And Mama will teach her how to promote people and write brilliant ads," she said with twinkling eyes.

Lang grinned at her. "Guess which things she's going to like learning best?"

Kirry pursed her lips and didn't say another word. Their daughter was going to have a very interesting life, and their marriage got better by the day. She looked back over the rocky road they'd traveled to this day and knew that she'd do it all over again. Her whole heart was in her eyes when she smiled at her husband; and in his when he smiled back.

*   *   *   *   *

Don't miss REGAN'S PRIDE
by Diana Palmer—it will lasso your heart in
April, 1994 and is available as Book #1000
in Silhouette Romance!

▼ SILHOUETTE®

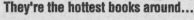
Desire™

They're the hottest books around...

With heroes you've grown to know—and *love*...

Created by Top authors—the ones *you* say are your favorites...

MAN OF THE MONTH: 1994

Don't miss a single one of these handsome hunks—

In January
Secret Agent Man
by *Diana Palmer*

In February
Wild Innocence
by *Ann Major*

In March
Wrangler's Lady
by *Jackie Merritt*

In April
Bewitched
by *Jennifer Greene*

In May
Lucy and the Stone
by *Dixie Browning*

In June
Haven's Call
by *Robin Elliott*

And that's just the first six months! Later in the year, look for books by Joan Hohl, Barbara Boswell, Cait London and Annette Broadrick.

Man of the Month...only from Silhouette Desire

As seen on TV!
Free Gift Offer

With a Free Gift proof-of-purchase from any Silhouette® book, you can receive a beautiful cubic zirconia pendant.

This gorgeous marquise-shaped stone is a genuine cubic zirconia—accented by an 18" gold tone necklace.

(Approximate retail value $19.95)

Send for yours today...
compliments of ▼ *Silhouette*®

To receive your free gift, a cubic zirconia pendant, send us one original proof-of-purchase, photocopies not accepted, from the back of any Silhouette Romance™, Silhouette Desire®, Silhouette Special Edition®, Silhouette Intimate Moments® or Silhouette Shadows™ title for January, February or March 1994 at your favorite retail outlet, together with the Free Gift Certificate, plus a check or money order for $2.50 (do not send cash) to cover postage and handling, payable to Silhouette Free Gift Offer. We will send you the specified gift. Allow 6 to 8 weeks for delivery. Offer good until March 31st, 1994 or while quantities last. Offer valid in the U.S. and Canada only.

Free Gift Certificate

Name: _____

Address: _____

City: _____ State/Province: _____ Zip/Postal Code: _____

Mail this certificate, one proof-of-purchase and a check or money order for postage and handling to: SILHOUETTE FREE GIFT OFFER 1994. In the U.S.: 3010 Walden Avenue, P.O. Box 9057, Buffalo NY 14269-9057. In Canada: P.O. Box 622, Fort Erie, Ontario L2Z 5X3

FREE GIFT OFFER   079-KBZ
ONE PROOF-OF-PURCHASE

To collect your fabulous FREE GIFT, a cubic zirconia pendant, you must include this original proof-of-purchase for each gift with the properly completed Free Gift Certificate.

079-KBZ